Nick DeSanto and Lorna Hathaway?

That was a joke.

For one thing, she didn't like him. She'd made that abundantly clear. But the overriding reason was they came from totally different worlds. Her wealth and position as an owner of the company he worked for was an insurmountable obstacle, even if he could win her over in person.

No. A relationship with Lorna was a pipe dream. It would never work. The best thing he could do now would be to disappear from her life.

That was his decision yesterday.... Yet after a restless night followed by a miserable day, he finally had to admit to himself that he didn't want to give her up. Even if he had to remain anonymous forever....

Dear Reader,

Get ready to counter the unpredictable weather outside with a lot of reading *inside*. And at Silhouette Special Edition we're happy to start you off with *Prescription: Love* by Pamela Toth, the next in our MONTANA MAVERICKS: GOLD RUSH GROOMS continuity. When a visiting medical resident—a gorgeous California girl—winds up assigned to Thunder Canyon General Hospital, she thinks of it as a temporary detour—until she meets the town's most eligible doctor! He soon has her thinking about settling down—permanently....

Crystal Green's *A Tycoon in Texas*, the next in THE FORTUNES OF TEXAS: REUNION continuity, features a workaholic businesswoman whose concentration is suddenly shaken by her devastatingly handsome new boss. Reader favorite Marie Ferrarella begins a new miniseries, THE CAMEO— about a necklace with special romantic powers—with *Because a Husband Is Forever*, in which a talk show hostess is coerced into taking on a bodyguard. Only, she had no idea he'd take his job title literally! In *Their Baby Miracle* by Lilian Darcy, a couple who'd called it quits months ago is brought back together by the premature birth of their child. Patricia Kay's *You've Got Game*, next in her miniseries THE HATHAWAYS OF MORGAN CREEK, gives us a couple who are constantly at each other's throats in real life—but their online relationship is another story altogether. And in *Picking Up the Pieces* by Barbara Gale, a world-famous journalist and a former top model risk scandal by following their hearts instead of their heads....

Enjoy them all, and please come back next month for six sensational romances, all from Silhouette Special Edition!

All the best,

Gail Chasan
Senior Editor

Please address questions and book requests to:
Silhouette Reader Service
U.S.: 3010 Walden Ave., P.O. Box 1325, Buffalo, NY 14269
Canadian: P.O. Box 609, Fort Erie, Ont. L2A 5X3

YOU'VE GOT GAME

PATRICIA KAY

Silhouette®

SPECIAL EDITION®

Published by Silhouette Books

America's Publisher of Contemporary Romance

Many thanks to Dee Williams of Bimbo Bakeries
USA for his kindness in giving my husband and me
a private tour of the Mrs. Baird's Bakery in Waco,
Texas, and for patiently answering all my questions.

 SILHOUETTE BOOKS

ISBN 0-373-24673-0

YOU'VE GOT GAME

Printed in U.S.A.

Books by Patricia Kay

Silhouette Special Edition

The Millionaire and the Mom #1387
†*Just a Small-Town Girl* #1437
Annie and the Confirmed Bachelor #1518
Secrets of a Small Town #1571
Man of the Hour #1629
††*Nanny in Hiding* #1642
††*His Best Friend* #1660
††*You've Got Game* #1673

Books previously published written as Trisha Alexander

Silhouette Special Edition

Cinderella Girl #640
When Somebody Loves You #748
When Somebody Needs You #784
Mother of the Groom #801
When Somebody Wants You #822
Here Comes the Groom #845
Say You Love Me #875
What Will the Children Think? #906
Let's Make It Legal #924
The Real Elizabeth Hollister... #940
The Girl Next Door #965
This Child Is Mine #989

*A Bride for Luke #1024
*A Bride for John #1047
*A Baby for Rebecca #1070
Stop the Wedding! #1097
Substitute Bride #1115
With this Wedding Ring #1169
A Mother for Jeffrey #1211
†*Wedding Bells and Mistletoe* #1289
†*Falling for an Older Man* #1308

†Callahans & Kin
††The Hathaways of Morgan Creek
*Three Brides and a Baby

PATRICIA KAY,
formerly writing as Trisha Alexander, is the *USA TODAY* bestselling author of more than thirty contemporary romances. She lives in Houston, Texas. To learn more about her, visit her Web site at www.patriciakay.com.

Chapter One

Lorna Hathaway stared at her monitor. She was stumped for a word. The only playable letters were *C*s, and no two-letter words existed using *C*.

She sighed and stretched. She'd been playing WordMaker for hours, a sad testament to her date-less life. But at least she was now playing against Coach1012, her favorite opponent, which almost made this frustrating impasse bearable.

Just then an instant message box popped up.

Hey, you having as much trouble as I am finding a word to play? Want to call a truce?

Coach1012 was being generous. He was ahead.

Sure, she wrote back. As long as you realize you're not doing me any favors, because if we keep playing, I'm sure to win.

Oh, really? he shot back, maybe we should keep playing then, take you down a peg or two....

She laughed and tried to think of a zinger in reply.

After a bit more banter, they agreed to quit the game. Even though Lorna's backside was sore from sitting so long, she waited. Sure enough, a few minutes later, her e-mail program dinged announcing that she had new mail. As anticipated, the sender was Coach1012. She opened the e-mail and began to read.

Hey, sweet stuff, playing against you tonight was fun. I needed something relaxing after that Little League game. We lost, 13 to 2. The kids don't care as much as the parents do, though. You should have heard 'em second-guessing me afterward. But criticism goes with the territory. You just gotta ignore it and remember it's not world peace or anything even close.

Anyway, you planning to play again tomorrow night?

Lorna had been debating whether she should tell her online buddy that she would be spending tomorrow supervising the packing of her belongings in preparation for a move to Houston, which was where Coach lived. She wanted to tell him, yet she hesitated.

She and Coach had become friends about six months earlier through the online game, and she enjoyed the friendship and competition between them. But the bottom line was, although they had discussed all kinds of personal likes and dislikes and had talked about their families and Lorna's divorce and Coach's dating life—even having discussions about religion and politics and the state of the world—they had never revealed identifying information about themselves.

The thing was, it was too easy to misrepresent yourself when your only contact was via the Internet, and as a single woman—not to mention, a wealthy single woman—Lorna knew she couldn't be too careful. She'd had enough bad experiences with men being more attracted to her money and position than they were to her—including her ex-husband—and she didn't intend to get burned again.

So up front, she'd told Coach she preferred remaining anonymous, and he'd agreed readily, which then made her wonder if he had something to hide. She'd laughed at herself, because he was probably wondering the same thing about *her.* She finally decided he'd also recognized the need for caution, and she respected that. It showed her he was a sensible man with a good head on his shoulders.

Her mind now made up, she answered saying she

would be out of town on business for a few days and probably wouldn't be online again until the following week. She ended the e-mail by adding that she'd see him then and signed the post with her online name, Sweet Stuff.

She'd no sooner logged off when her cell phone rang. The caller ID showed the caller to be her younger sister Claudia.

"Hey!" Lorna said, smiling. "Thought you were going to the Astros game tonight."

"I didn't feel like it—I'm really tired, and I've got a cold coming on, I think—so I told John to go without me."

"Wow, you must *really* feel lousy if you're willing to let your new husband out of your sight for an entire evening," Lorna teased.

"I made sure he wore his ball and chain."

Lorna laughed. The truth was, John Renzo had fallen in love with Claudia at first sight and been crazy about her ever since. There wasn't much danger he'd have a roving eye.

"So are you ready for the big move?" Claudia asked.

"As ready as I'll ever be."

"I'm so glad you're coming to Houston. It'll be great having you here. I've missed you."

"I've missed you, too."

"No second thoughts?"

Lorna had had a lot of second thoughts because

she loved her job as CFO of Hathaway Baking Company, and she would miss being close to her brother Bryce and his wife Amy and their children, but none of her reservations had changed her mind.

"No. I still think this is the right thing for me to do. If I hope to meet someone and have any kind of personal life of my own, I need to get out of Morgan Creek."

"I know."

Claudia *did* know. The lack of eligible men in their small hometown was one of the reasons she'd moved away herself a year ago.

"I don't know, Lorna, I just—"

"What?"

"Well, after all you've told me about him, I can't help worrying that you won't be able to stand working with Nick DeSanto."

Lorna grimaced. She was trying not to think about the fact that she would have to interact with Nick De-Santo every day. Nick was the plant manager of the Houston division of Hathaway Baking Company, and a more frustrating man would be hard to find. "I can handle him."

"You keep saying that, but every time you've been around him, he's managed to get under your skin."

"I know, but that's been my fault as much as his. You don't have to personally like someone to work with them. Bryce says Nick does a first-class job running the plant, and that's the important thing."

"And you won't be working *for* him."

"No." If Lorna had had to work under Nick, this move wouldn't be happening. But she wouldn't. She would report directly to the new CFO in Morgan Creek.

Later, in bed for the night, Lorna reminded herself that everything in life was a choice, and that there were always trade-offs to be made. She knew being the combination business manager/office manager at a satellite plant wasn't comparable to the position she held at the Morgan Creek headquarters of her family's company, but her job wasn't going to keep her warm at night, nor would it give her the baby she craved.

Thinking about a baby, she felt the old, familiar ache. She wanted a child more than anything, and her desire had only gotten stronger since the birth of her newest niece six weeks earlier. Lorna had just turned thirty-four, and she knew she didn't have forever. If she was going to have a baby of her own, she needed to get busy. And the first order of business was finding a man she could love and respect, one who really loved her and who wanted a family as much as she did.

That's why you're moving. So stop worrying. You've made your decision, and it's a good one. It might not be easy, but this will work. You'll make it work. And if Nick DeSanto gives you any trouble, you'll give him trouble right back.

"So…Nick. What do you think about the Texans chance of makin' the playoffs this year?"

Nick DeSanto looked at his brother Jay, who was helping himself to meatballs from the serving bowl in the center of the dinner table. "What'd you say?"

Jay frowned. "What's with you today? You're a million miles away. That's about the third time I've said something and you haven't been listening."

Nick shrugged. "Sorry. I was thinking about work."

"You're always thinking about work," his brother Mike piped in. He twirled his fork in his spaghetti, then lifted the enormous mound to his mouth. Before popping it in, he added, "Give it a rest, why doncha?"

The entire DeSanto family always had Sunday dinner together at the home of Nick's parents, Mike, Sr., and Carmela, and this Sunday was no exception. Normally Nick liked Sunday afternoons. He could relax and be himself with his family, and his mother was still the best cook in the world. But today he couldn't manage to stop thinking about the imminent arrival of Lorna Hathaway at the satellite baking company plant where he had been the manager for the past seven years.

Why the hell was she coming to Houston to take

a lesser position than the one she'd held at the main office? This was the question that had bugged the hell out of Nick ever since Bryce Hathaway had called him a month ago to tell him his sister Lorna was coming.

You know damn well why she's coming. For some reason, the Hathaways don't trust you. She's coming to spy.

Nick hated thinking this, but what other reason could there be? *Or maybe they're getting ready to push you out and put her in your place.* He frowned and drank some of his iced tea.

"Are you having a problem at work, Nicky?" his mother asked. Her blue eyes studied him thoughtfully.

"No, Ma, no problem." If Nick admitted he was worried about Lorna Hathaway's arrival at the plant, his mother would worry, too, and he didn't want that. He was a big boy. He could handle his own problems.

"Are you sure?" she pressed.

"Yeah, everything's fine."

"Hey, Nicky, you still dating that Kirsten?"

The question came from Nick's sister Marie.

He shook his head and ate some of his spaghetti, hoping she'd drop the subject.

No such luck.

"You go through girlfriends the way the kids go through soft drinks," Marie said.

"Yeah, Nick, when you gonna settle down?" his father said. "Find yourself a nice Italian girl like your mother and have some nice Italian kids?"

Marie started to laugh. "Pop, you're hilarious. Nicky hasn't dated an Italian girl since he was in high school."

She looked as if she wanted to say something else about the women he dated, but her two boys were avidly listening, so Nick figured she'd thought better of it. Jeez, he hated it when his family started in on him.

"Leave Nicky alone," his mother said. "He's only thirty-eight. He's got plenty of time."

Marie hooted. "Plenty of time! Jeez, Ma, you couldn't *wait* for me to get married, and I was barely twenty-three!"

"It's different for a girl," Carmela said. Daintily, she cut up her meatball.

"Why is it different?"

Nick stifled a grin. Marie was getting mad, and it amused him. It took so little to fire up his sister's temper.

"Because in spite of what lots of women think, it's not so easy to have babies when you're in your thirties. It's best to have them by the time you're twenty-five. That's when you're the most fertile." So saying, Nick's mother continued eating.

"Oh, for heaven's sake, Ma. Today women are having babies well into their forties."

Carmela shook her head. "Not smart, in my opinion. Just think, if you wait till you're forty to have a baby, you're almost sixty before he's out of high school."

"So?" Marie said.

"So it's crazy," her mother retorted. "There's no way I could cope with a teenager at my age."

"Ma, you have more energy than me and Rich put together," Marie said, nudging her husband, who nodded in agreement.

Carmela smiled.

Nick mentally rolled his eyes. His family was a constant source of amusement and frustration.

"Can we please change the subject?" Jay said. "Could we talk about something interesting? Like baseball."

"Oh, you always want to talk about sports," his wife Kathy said with a grimace.

Lost in the shuffle of his family's good-natured bickering, Nick went back to planning strategy for when Lorna Hathaway came to town.

First thing he'd do was let her know he was on to her. And the second thing he'd do was update his résumé. But even as he thought this, he knew it would be difficult—if not impossible—to find another job in his field at his current level. The downturn in the economy had affected every business, and the food business was no exception. Even in the best of times, it wouldn't have been a cakewalk to make that kind of change.

He was still thinking about this disturbing turn of events later that evening when he arrived at his Heights-area home. But almost immediately, his mood lifted. The house always had that effect on him. He'd bought the old Victorian as a fixer-upper five years earlier to the dismay of his family, who couldn't understand why he wanted a house that was falling down around him.

"Nicky," his mom had said, "why don't you buy yourself a new house? You can afford it."

"Because I like old houses, Ma," he'd explained patiently.

"But *why?* Don't you want a nice, big shower and modern plumbing?"

"I'll eventually have those things."

But she'd just shaken her head—although recently, she'd admitted she'd been wrong and told him the house was turning out to be beautiful.

It hadn't been easy or cheap. Since the day he'd bought the house, every extra penny Nick could come up with had been poured into it. The house still wasn't perfect, but it was slowly becoming what he'd envisioned it being the first time he laid eyes on it. He'd done most of the work himself, although his brothers lent a hand whenever they had any spare time.

Now the newly repaired wooden floors gleamed with stain and polish, and the walls were resplendent with fresh coats of paint and updated wallpaper. All the window glass was new, too, except for the stained-glass panels on either side of the front door, which had somehow survived the previous owners' neglect. The only major work that remained was re-modeling the kitchen, which still had its original chipped porcelain sink and a 1940s vintage Roper gas stove.

As he walked inside, Maggie, his year-old choc-olate Lab, bounded down the hall to greet him. Kneeling, he rubbed her ears. "Have you been good while I was gone, Maggie, girl?"

In answer, she licked his chin.

He laughed. "C'mon, I know you want to go out."

Tail wagging, she followed him to the kitchen. He unlocked the back door and let her out. Opening the refrigerator, he took out a cold bottle of beer. Then he leaned against the counter and slowly drank as he waited for Maggie to finish her business and ask to come back inside. His thoughts once more turned to Lorna Hathaway.

Damn. Why was it that things could never run smoothly? Someone always had to throw a monkey wrench into the works and screw things up.

Well, he knew one thing for sure. He might have to find another job, but he wasn't going to go quietly.

And if Lorna Hathaway thought differently, she had a big shock coming, because he intended to give her one helluva fight.

* * *

"Careful," Lorna cautioned, heart banging in alarm as the movers strained under the weight of her baby grand piano. She knew it might be a tight fit getting the piano into the living room of the bungalow she'd purchased in Houston, yet there was no way she was going to leave it behind.

She sighed. She liked the small house she'd bought in West University Place, only one block from where Claudia and John lived, but she hated saying goodbye to her house here—a gorgeous Victorian that she'd restored to its original beauty in the ten years since she'd purchased it.

With the house, she always thought in terms of "she," even though she and her ex, Keith, had bought the house together and moved in as newlyweds. Keith, however, had never loved it the way Lorna did. He'd have preferred something new in one of the gated communities closer to Austin where up-and-coming executives lived.

He'd given in because it was Lorna's money that enabled them to buy a house in the first place. But he had no real interest in their home, and she was the one who'd lovingly supervised the workmen, who'd replaced the faulty electrical wiring and the worn-out plumbing. She was the one who'd scrubbed and polished and painted on weekends and evenings when Keith was golfing or working late. And she was the one who'd haunted antique shops and weekend flea markets to find just the right pieces of furniture to create the tranquility and elegance she envisioned.

She swallowed against the lump in her throat. She was giving up so much to make the move to Houston. Again, doubts assailed her. She imagined most people would think she was crazy.

"Do *you* think I'm crazy, Buttercup?" she whispered. In answer, the calico cat in her arms made a sound halfway between a purr and a meow.

Just then a white SUV pulled up in front of the house across the street. Lorna smiled as she watched her sister-in-law Amy climb out and wave, then open the back door where she removed the newest addition to hers and Bryce's family from her baby carrier. Lorna put Buttercup down on the porch railing and waited on the top step.

"Emily and I thought we'd come and see how you're doing," Amy said when she and the baby joined Lorna on the porch.

Lorna reached for the chubby infant, relishing the feel of her warm, sweet skin as she nuzzled the baby's neck, then settled her into her arms. "Oh, you're so beautiful." Emily made a contented sound. "She's such a sweetheart, Amy."

Amy smiled happily. "She *is*, isn't she? The girls just adore her."

Amy had a five-year-old daughter from her first

marriage and Bryce's two daughters from *his* first marriage were nine and ten, so she had her hands full.

"Speaking of the girls, where are they?"

"You forgot. Today's the first day of school."

"I *did* forget, and I even saw the school bus this morning."

"Well, you've had lots of things on your mind."

"So Calista started kindergarten today?"

Amy grinned. "Yes, and she was thrilled to be going to school like her big sisters."

Calista had worshiped Susan and Stella from the very first day Amy had entered their lives, and in turn, they were crazy about her.

"She picked out her own outfit, too," Amy said. By now the two women had settled onto the swing and were gently moving back and forth. Buttercup settled in her favorite loaf-of-bread position on top of the railing and watched them.

"What did she choose?"

"Green shorts and that white peasant blouse you bought her."

Lorna grinned. "She has good taste."

They continued to talk about the children, with Amy bringing Lorna up-to-date on the older girls' doings.

"Emily's asleep," Amy observed a few minutes later.

Lorna looked down at the baby. She was so utterly precious, this little goddaughter of hers. Her tiny mouth was open, her breathing shallow and occasionally her eyelids fluttered. Lorna swallowed against the sudden lump in her throat.

As if she knew exactly what Lorna was thinking, Amy reached over and squeezed her arm.

Lorna willed herself to stay dry-eyed.

"I should be going," Amy said. "You're coming for dinner later, right?"

Lorna nodded.

"Are you still planning to leave for Houston sometime tomorrow?"

"Yes. The movers are delivering my things Friday, and I need to be there."

Amy stood. "And the Baxters are moving in here on Monday?"

Mark Baxter was the newly hired sales manager at the plant, and he and his wife Leslie had purchased Lorna's home. She'd been lucky to find a buyer so quickly, and she knew it. "Yes." Lorna handed Amy the baby, who barely stirred. "They're really nice, Amy. I think you'll like them. In fact, I can see you and Leslie Baxter becoming good friends."

Amy smiled sadly. "No one can take your place."

"Or yours," Lorna said softly.

After Amy left, it only took the movers another hour or so to finish loading all of Lorna's belongings. Once they were gone, Lorna—followed by Buttercup—walked back inside to survey what was left to do. There wasn't much, thank goodness. The only pieces of furniture that remained were ones Lorna didn't have room for in the new house, and the Baxters had decided to buy. Everything else had either been disposed of before the movers arrived or had been loaded onto the truck for transport to Houston. Tomorrow morning Lorna had a cleaning service coming. After that, she would be free to leave.

Free to begin my new life.

Suddenly, the melancholy that had plagued her all day began to lift and Lorna smiled.

Everything really *was* going to be okay. She could feel it in her bones.

And who knew?

Maybe by this time next year, she would be well on her way to having the kind of life she'd dreamed of all along.

Chapter Two

"Lorna, I love your house!" Claudia plopped onto Lorna's sofa and stretched her long legs out in front of her.

Lorna glanced around with a smile. It was the Wednesday after her move-in, and she was in good shape, with almost everything unpacked and put away. "It *is* looking good, isn't it? You know, at first I thought I would have a hard time getting used to having a much smaller place than I had at home, but I'm finding I like it. It's cozy."

Claudia grinned. "It *is* cozy. In fact, it's ador-able. And Buttercup seems to like her new surroundings, too." She looked over at the cat, who was curled up on the hearth, even though it would be months before it might be cold enough to build a fire.

"Yes, she settled right in as if she'd lived here forever. Didn't you, Buttercup?"

The cat never even turned her head.

Claudia laughed. "Don't you love how cats totally ignore you unless *they* want something?"

Lorna smiled. "So what brings you here so early? I thought your last class wasn't over until three." The new semester at Bayou City College, where Claudia taught business and marketing courses, had just begun.

"I had a doctor's appointment, so I rescheduled today's classes."

"Nothing's wrong, I hope."

Claudia grinned. "No, nothing's wrong. Just the opposite, in fact."

From her sister's expression, Lorna had a pretty good idea of what was coming.

"I'm pregnant," Claudia said, her smile filling her entire face.

"Oh, sweetie, that's *wonderful!* I'm so happy for you!"

"And I want you to be our baby's godmother," Claudia bubbled on. "Well, actually, I thought we'd have two godmothers. You and John's sister Jennifer." She jumped up from the couch and hugged

Lorna. "Oh, Lorna, I'm so happy! I never knew I could *be* so happy!"

Laughing and squealing, the sisters danced around the room together.

"Does John know yet?" Lorna asked when they'd finally settled down again.

"Of course. I called him right away. He's totally thrilled."

"He'll make a wonderful father."

"He *will*, won't he?" Now Claudia's smile turned tender.

Lorna wondered if Claudia had any idea how much she envied her. How much she wanted a baby, too. They hadn't discussed the subject recently, because Lorna didn't want her sister feeling sorry for her or feeling as if she had to censor everything she said in deference to Lorna's sensibilities, so maybe she imagined Lorna had given up on the idea. "When are you due?"

"The doctor said about the middle of April."

"Perfect. You'll beat the summer heat."

"I know. I couldn't have planned it better if I'd tried."

"So you *weren't* trying?"

Claudia laughed. "You know what I mean."

Lorna smiled affectionately. "Yes, I do. I was only teasing you."

They talked baby plans for a while, then Claudia

said, "Telling you about the baby isn't the only reason I dropped by today."

"Oh?"

"I wanted to invite you to go out with us Saturday night."

"That's sweet of you, but you and John will want to celebrate your good news by yourselves. I'd just be a fifth wheel."

"No, you won't. Anyway, we'll be double-dating."

Lorna made a face. "Oh, Claudia, not a blind date."

"Don't say it like that."

"I can't help it. I hate blind dates."

"Jonah's great. He's a cameraman and works for John's company. He's a bit younger than you are, but he's lots of fun and cute, and I think you'll like him."

Lorna grimaced. "Younger?"

"Not *that* much. Maybe a couple of years. Anyway, what's the big deal?"

"I'm not good with younger guys."

Claudia just rolled her eyes.

Actually, Lorna wasn't good at dating, period. And she was especially bad at blind dates.

"Why are you always putting yourself down?"

"I'm not. I just…oh, you know. I never know what to say when I first meet a guy. I always feel like I'm boring them to death." *Like I bored Keith.*

"Oh, Lorna, that's ridiculous. You're smart and beautiful and funny. Why would they be bored?"

"I might be smart, but I'm certainly not beautiful, and funny is still up for a vote."

"See? There you go again. Putting yourself down."

"Being honest isn't putting myself down."

"I swear, Keith did a real job on you, didn't he?"

"Well, you've got to admit that finding out your husband prefers a silicone-breasted cheerleader barely out of high school and who can't talk about anything more complicated than who's dating who in Hollywood doesn't do a lot to build your confidence."

"Keith is an idiot."

"I won't argue with you there, but the fact remains he lost interest in me as soon as he realized he would have to work for my money." Lorna wasn't bitter. The truth was the truth. She'd misjudged Keith. She'd thought he really loved her, that her money wasn't a factor in his courtship. She'd been wrong.

"Like I said, he's an idiot," Claudia said. "Anyway, back to Saturday night. We thought we'd go see a movie—maybe that new one with Drew Barrymore—it's supposed to be hilarious, then go out for dinner. John and I discovered this really good Cajun place, and on Saturday nights they have a zydeco band."

"Oh, Claudia, I don't know...."

"Lorna, I'm not going to take no for an answer. You're going, and that's that. We've already told Jonah all about you, and he's excited about meeting you."

"If he's so great, why does he need a blind date?"

Claudia shook her head in exasperation. "Honestly, Lorna, sometimes I just want to choke you."

Lorna grinned.

"That's better. Now say you'll go."

"Oh, okay, I'll go."

"Good. I'll let you know what time after I talk to John. Now, tell me, have you visited the plant yet?"

"No, but I thought I'd pop in tomorrow just to say hello and meet the office staff."

"You're starting work on Monday?"

"Yes."

Lorna had been going to take a couple of weeks off, then had decided one was enough. Besides, she was anxious to get started on her new job.

Claudia stood. Lorna couldn't help studying her belly, exposed by her low-riding pants and cropped top. So far, she didn't look any different than she'd always looked, which was fantastic. She grinned at the glint of silver. "How long are you going to wear that navel ring?"

Claudia laughed. "John likes it, but I plan to take it out when I start to show." She slung her handbag over her shoulder. "Walk out with me?"

Lorna stood on the front stoop and waved goodbye until Claudia's Jeep disappeared around the corner. Then she slowly walked back inside. Her shoulders sagged. She was happy for Claudia, *thrilled* for Claudia. But a part of her ached with the knowledge that even her baby sister had passed her by. That it was only she, Lorna, who had failed at marriage and was still childless.

Would motherhood ever happen for her? she wondered forlornly. Or was she forever doomed to be just an aunt or a godmother to her siblings' children?

For the rest of the day, she fought against a rising melancholy. Finally, knowing the only way to stop the negative emotions was to lose herself in something she loved, she headed for the piano. It hadn't been tuned since the move—something she had planned to take care of immediately—but today she didn't care.

Minutes later, she was deep into the lilting waterfall of Rachmaninoff's Piano Concerto no. 1 in F-sharp Minor and the rest of the world fell away.

Nick was on the plant floor supervising the installation of a new bagging machine when his secretary paged him. Telling Jim Hennessey, his maintenance manager, he'd be right back, Nick walked out to the distribution center where it wasn't as noisy.

"Yeah?" he said when he had Karen on the phone.

"Miss Hathaway's here," she said.

"What? What the hell is she doing here?" he muttered. "She doesn't start until Monday."

Ignoring his irritated response, she chirped, "Would you like me to show her around? Or do you want to come up and do it yourself?"

Nick knew Lorna Hathaway was probably close enough to hear what Karen had to say. He swore under his breath. "I'll be there in a few minutes."

"You go on, Nick," Jim said when Nick rejoined him. "I can finish this up."

Nick exhaled a frustrated breath. "Thanks." He stripped off his work gloves and the hairnet everyone had to wear on the plant floor, then headed toward the metal stairs that led to the next level where all the offices were located.

When he reached his office he told himself not to show his irritation. To be polite and businesslike. But one look at the haughty ice queen wearing a dress that probably cost more than he made in a week and thumbing through the second quarter report, and all Nick's good resolutions flew out the window. He didn't know what it was about Lorna Hathaway that got under his skin so bad, but he couldn't stand her. She was the epitome of the type of woman who had always looked down her nose at Nick and his brothers. The kind that knew he was from the wrong side of the tracks and thought he should have stayed there.

"You should have called first," he said.

Her head snapped up. Something flashed in her eyes, but was gone in a second. "Nice to see you, too," she said evenly.

He almost smiled. She might be a snob, but she

wasn't stupid. "Thing is, I'm a little busy today. The cooler was on the fritz for two hours earlier this morning, which backed everything up, so now we're behind. Added to that, we're installing a new outer-bagging machine, and that's put us even more behind. So this is a real bad time. Maybe you and I could reschedule?"

"I'm sorry about the problems. However, I only dropped into your office as a courtesy," she said, rising. "I actually came to meet *my* staff."

He frowned. "Staff? You don't have a staff."

She stared at him. "But Nan had a secretary—her name was Stella, I believe—and I know there were at least two clerks the last time I was here. And the bookkeeper."

Nan Mackey was their former business manager, the one Lorna was replacing.

"Stella quit when Nan left. She was pregnant. Stella, that is. And the two clerks were temps. We were in the middle of inventory the last time you were here. Phyllis, the bookkeeper, telecommutes, only coming in at the end of the month or for meetings."

"I see. Well…have you done anything about replacing Stella?"

He shrugged. "No. I figured you'd rather hire your own secretary." *Someone you can count on to help sabotage me.* "Not take someone I chose for you."

She nodded. "Yes, you're right, although I would

have much preferred to have Stella, since she would have been a big help to me. I don't suppose there's anyone else here who might fill the bill?"

"Nope. Not that I know of." He looked at Karen. "You know anyone who aspires to the office, Karen?"

She frowned in thought. "I could ask around. Maybe Rita?"

"I can't spare Rita. She's my best line-supervisor."

"Yolanda?"

He shook his head. "Not Yolanda, either."

Karen shrugged. "Well, they're the only two I can think of."

"Sorry," he said to Lorna. "Maybe you'd like to bring someone over from the Morgan Hills plant."

She just looked at him. "You know I can't do that."

"Hey, you're one of the owners. You can do anything you want." *Whether it's kosher or not.*

For a moment, she didn't answer. Then, coolly, she said, "Can we step into your office, please?"

"I only have a few minutes." He walked over and opened the door, motioning her through. Then he closed it firmly behind him. "Have a seat." After she was seated, he perched on the edge of his desk, knowing that height always gave an advantage. He waited. If she had something to say, let her say it.

"Look, Nick, can we call a truce?"

"What do you mean?"

"I mean just what I said. Let's agree that we don't much like each other. That's fine. I don't need for everyone to like me. However, we do have to work together, so can we also agree to be civil and courteous to one another?"

"Sure."

She seemed taken aback by his ready agreement. "Good. Then you'll not be making any more remarks like the one you just made in front of your secretary, right?"

"What was uncivil or discourteous about that? It's the truth, isn't it?"

Now she bristled, sitting up and tensing like a cat ready to strike. Her eyes, normally an icy blue, blazed. "No, it wasn't the truth. When have I *ever* thrown my weight around?"

"Could it have been when you and your brother decided you'd replace Nan without consulting me or even asking me if I had a problem with it?"

That took the starch out of her sails. "I…" Her voice trailed off, and she sank back in her chair. Her gaze met his. "I'm sorry. I didn't realize Bryce *hadn't* consulted you. And you're right. He should have. We *both* should have."

Nick shrugged. "Apology accepted." He stood. "But you really should have called before coming over today, because I've got a full schedule. If you want to look around on your own, though, you're welcome to do it. But if you can wait till Monday, I'll show you everything you need to know to get started."

She nodded. "Fine." She stood, too. "Seeing as how I have no staff to meet, I guess I'll wait until Monday. In the meantime, would you ask Karen to find a temp for me until I can get someone hired?"

"Why don't you talk to Karen about that? That way she'll know exactly what you want."

"Okay. I just didn't want to step on your toes."

"No problem."

Nick watched as she walked out of his office. She might have tried to disarm him with an apology, but she was a tight-ass if he'd ever seen one. No wonder her husband had left her. Nick could just imagine the way she'd lorded it over the poor guy and made him toe the line. No man with any pride could live like that.

Well, she'd met her match now. Nick wanted to keep his job, but he wouldn't grovel before Lorna Hathaway in order to do so. And the sooner she knew that, the better.

But even as he told himself this, he felt the stirring of a grudging admiration for the way she'd handled herself today. At the very least, having her at the plant promised to be interesting.

Damn, damn, damn, damn.
Lorna mentally kicked herself for not calling Nick

before going to the plant, but mostly she was furious with herself for not doing her homework.

She should have *known* the only "staff" she'd have would be a secretary. Why hadn't she thought to check before opening her mouth? Instead, she'd just assumed that the people she'd seen on her last trip to Houston were permanent employees.

You know what they say about making assumptions, don't you?

Now Nick DeSanto not only didn't like her because she was part of the Hathaway family—at least she *thought* that's why he didn't like her—but he probably also thought she was lazy or careless or worse—stupid.

Well, it was her own fault if he did, and she would have to work doubly hard to correct that impression.

And topping everything off was the glaring omission Nick had pointed out—that neither she nor Bryce had asked him if he would have a problem with her taking the business manager's job. In Nick's shoes, she'd be furious. She'd think that they didn't value him as an employee, which she knew wasn't true. Bryce had recently told her he considered Nick DeSanto the best of his seven plant managers.

Lorna sighed.

Not exactly the best way to begin. Not the best way at all.

* * *

Nick never got home Friday night. He worked straight through until Saturday morning when they finally got back on schedule. He was exhausted and was sure Cal Lopez, his production manager, who'd also worked a twenty-four-hour stretch, was equally exhausted.

That was the trouble with running at full production capacity. There was no wiggle room, no way to make up downtime from equipment problems. As it was, each of the ninety nonoffice personnel put in anywhere from fifty to sixty hour workweeks. For months now, they'd been running three shifts a day, ten hours per shift.

So when they had a serious problem on the line, they lost money, because some orders could not be filled.

Nick knew it was time to expand the plant, and he was pretty sure Bryce Hathaway knew it, too. Soon they would have to discuss the pros and cons, and Nick imagined Lorna Hathaway would have to be included in the discussions.

But that was a problem for another day.

Today, after getting at least eight hours of uninterrupted sleep, the most complicated decision he intended to make was where to take his date for dinner tonight.

* * *

Lorna tried on ten different outfits before she decided on slim black pants and a sheer rose-colored blouse worn over a deeper rose tube top. She wished she hadn't agreed to go on this date. She'd never yet had a blind date that was more than bearable. Why had she allowed Claudia to pressure her into saying yes?

Staring at herself in the mirror, she wondered what this Jonah person would think when he saw her. She knew she was too tall and too skinny. And she had no boobs. Well, not enough to speak of, anyway.

"I'm not sexy," she muttered aloud.

Tonight's date probably imagined she looked like Claudia, who *was* sexy. Well, he was bound to be disappointed, and then the evening wouldn't even be bearable.

It would be miserable.

I'll call Claudia and tell her I'm sick.

Lorna was halfway to the phone when she knew she couldn't do it. First of all, Claudia wouldn't believe her. And then she and John would be put in the really impossible position of having to lie to John's friend.

Lorna sighed heavily and headed into the bathroom to put on her makeup. As she tried to decide whether to tie her hair back loosely or leave it down, she told herself that no matter what happened tonight, this was the absolute last time she'd ever allow anyone to talk her into a blind date.

Yes, she wanted to meet men.

And yes, she knew she'd have to go through the dating ritual no matter how much she hated the entire scenario.

But she would do so on her own terms. She'd join a church that had a singles group and she'd sign up for some classes in things that interested her and she'd get involved in some community activities.

That was the way to meet people and get to know them gradually. Not on a blind date.

Jonah Whitfield turned out to be a pretty nice guy, and Lorna found herself relaxing once she realized he wasn't a smart-ass or one of those guys who think they're God's gift to women. In fact, by the time they reached Burney's, the restaurant Claudia had mentioned, and were seated over drinks, Lorna was actually enjoying herself. And the zydeco band was great, especially the fiddle player. Lorna got a kick out of watching the people do some kind of line dance that looked like lots of fun.

"Want to try it?" Jonah said, turning to her.

"I'm a terrible dancer."

"Oh, you are not!" Claudia said. "C'mon, we'll all go out there and try it."

The dance turned out to be as much fun as Lorna had imagined, and she didn't screw up too badly. At any rate, by the time it was over, she was managing to follow fairly easily. It was only as she and Jonah were walking back to their table that she saw Nick DeSanto. Her mouth dropped open. Their gazes locked, and she knew he was as startled to see her as she was to see him. For a second, she wasn't sure he was going to acknowledge her, but then he raised his hand in a salute. She gave him a little wave in return and quickly turned her attention back to Jonah. She felt awkward until they reached their table, certain Nick was watching her.

She couldn't believe it. Why, with all the places there were in Houston, did Nick DeSanto have to turn up *here?*

"Somebody you know?" Jonah asked, looking in Nick's direction.

"Just someone from work." Surreptitiously she tried to see who Nick's date was. Oh, of course. She should have known. He was with a busty redhead who wore a short, tight white skirt and skimpy green top that hugged her breasts and bared her midriff. The band was now playing a romantic ballad and as Lorna watched, the two of them got up to dance.

"You want to dance to this?" Jonah said.

Lorna shook her head. All the couples on the floor, including Claudia and John, who were still out there, looked glued together. Nick and his redhead were no exception. Lorna quickly averted her eyes. The last thing she wanted was for him to see her watching him.

The remainder of the evening was excruciating, although she did her best not to show it. After all, it wasn't Jonah's fault Nick DeSanto was here. But she couldn't help wishing Jonah were different, that he didn't wear his long hair in a ponytail, and that he didn't look as if he were ten years younger than she. Why what Nick thought about her or her date was important to her, she didn't know. She only knew she wished she were with someone older and more sophisticated.

And then, just when Lorna thought she couldn't stand another minute of pretending to be having a wonderful time, Nick and his date left. Lorna hadn't realized just how tense she was until they walked out the door.

Even so, the evening had been ruined for her, and she couldn't wait until it was time to go home. When Claudia yawned and looked at her watch, saying, "It's almost midnight, and I'm tired. Do you mind if we go?" Lorna couldn't agree fast enough.

There was another awkward moment when Jonah walked her to her door, when she was afraid he'd want to kiss her good-night, but all he did was grin and say he'd had fun and hoped to see her again.

"Thank you," Lorna said, knowing she'd make an excuse if he called her.

And then he was gone, and she was blessedly

alone. Finally she was free to think about the evening—especially about seeing Nick. She wished it hadn't happened. She didn't know why, but she couldn't help feeling having Nick see her at the restaurant with Jonah had put her at a disadvantage.

And yet there was a part of her that wondered if he'd thought she looked attractive tonight. Why she cared, she couldn't have said. She certainly wasn't *interested* in Nick. Not only would she never date someone she worked with, but Nick DeSanto was not her type.

Not by a long shot.

Forget about him, she told herself as she climbed into bed. *What he thinks is not important.*

"Want to come in?" Cherry said in her low, sexy drawl. There was subtext written into every word.

Nick shook his head. "Thanks, but I'm driving over to Lake Charles in the morning, and I need to get an early start." That was true, but in the past it wouldn't have stopped him from the spending the night with a sexy number like Cherry.

"Are you sure?" She moved closer, putting her arms around his neck.

"It's tempting," he said gallantly, "but I can't." For some reason, he just wasn't in the mood tonight.

Cherry pouted. "You're no fun." She continued to

wheedle, but he remained firm, and finally she stopped trying to get him to change his mind.

Later, as he drove home, he thought about how he hadn't been in the mood for a long time now. He never would have confessed it to his mother *or* his sister, but Nick was tired of the dating scene. He was ready for a committed relationship, but some days he wondered if he'd ever find the right kind of woman.

What he wanted was the kind of woman who would not only fit in with his family, but who was smart and interesting *and* sexy. Someone who was a match for him, who would give as good as she got. Someone he could respect.

For some reason, his thoughts turned to Lorna Hathaway. Not that *she* was his kind of woman. Not even close. Still, he had to admit she'd surprised him tonight. He never would have imagined the ice queen could look so…*hot*. He'd noticed her long before she'd seen him. Watching her dance with that young guy, he'd been amazed. She'd shown a side of herself Nick hadn't known existed.

Nick fell asleep wondering how he could use what he'd learned about Lorna Hathaway tonight to his advantage.

Chapter Three

FROM: Coach1012@bayoucity.net
TO: SweetStuff@jamboree.net
DATE: 30 August
SUBJECT: Home Yet?

Hey, girl, it's been a week since I've heard from you or seen you online. Thought you were only going to be gone a few days? Hate to admit it, but I've been a little worried. Hope nothing's wrong. Everything here's about the same, except the Little League season is finally over for our team. You know I love coaching, but I'm always glad when I get a break, especially when I have a season like this one has been. Those poor kids. They only won two games, came in last in their division. But I told them they'd be better next year and even better after that, so I don't think they were too bummed.

Since the season ended, I've been working like a dog. We've had all kinds of problems here, but things seem to be okay for now. Anyway, if you're back from your business trip and can make it on-line tonight, I'll try to be there by eight. If not, I guess I'll just have to wait until I hear from you. Your buddy,
C.

Lorna felt a pang of guilt. She'd been so busy the past week, she hadn't logged on to WordMaker since the night she'd told Coach she had to go away on business, nor had she e-mailed him. She decided to zap him a quick reply.

FROM: SweetStuff@jamboree.net
TO: Coach1012@bayoucity.net
DATE: 30 August
SUBJECT: Re: Home Yet?
Hi, Coach. Sorry I've been gone so long. Things got hectic here and I've been so tired at night, I haven't had the energy to read, let alone play WordMaker. This is the first time I've been on Jam-

boree in days. But I've got my life under control
again—as under control as life can ever be! <g>
Anyway, I'll log on at eight tonight. Send me an
IM and let me know which room you're in.
See you later!
SS

She smiled to think he'd been worrying about her.
Once again, she felt bad about not telling him she had
relocated to Houston. He seemed like such a nice
guy. Maybe she *should* tell him.

But even as she considered it, she knew she'd
made the right decision. At least for now. Maybe one
of these days, she'd take the plunge. But she was
afraid once he knew they were in the same city, he'd
suggest getting together. Even the thought of meeting him gave her a case of butterflies. She knew it
was cowardly, but she wanted to hang on to her fantasy of him as a certain kind of person, and once they
met, she'd finally have to face reality.

What if she couldn't stand him? That would be
awful because right now she treasured their friendship, and she'd hate to lose it.

Talking to Coach was like having a shrink. He was
a safe place to vent or discuss things that bothered
her because he didn't know who she was and the
things she said couldn't come back to haunt her.

But if they *knew* each other—really knew each

other—that would all change. Their relationship might end up being better, but it *could* end up being much worse. In fact, she could lose him altogether.

And that was what scared Lorna.

Right now Coach was important to her. Meeting him at night to play WordMaker and talk was something she could look forward to, especially when she was having a bad day. She didn't want to lose that.

You really are *a coward.*

She bit her lip. How could she ever expect to fulfill her dreams and desires if she was afraid to take a chance? The question disturbed her, because she had never thought of herself that way. In fact, until Keith had left her, she'd never *been* a coward. She'd been adventurous and brave. She remembered how she'd bucked her entire family and followed her first serious boyfriend to Florida State, where he had a football scholarship, instead of going to an Ivy League school, as her mother had wanted, or the University of Texas, as her grandmother had wanted.

Unfortunately, when Keith walked out on her, he had taken a big chunk of her self-confidence with him. Suddenly, she'd questioned her entire self-worth. But she was getting better. She'd taken a big chance by moving to Houston, and soon maybe she'd be ready to take a chance on Coach, too.

She hoped so, because she knew it was time.

Later, over brunch with Claudia and John, Claudia said, "You're awfully quiet today."

Lorna blinked. She'd been thinking about Coach again and wondering if she should tell Claudia and John about him, maybe get their opinion of the situation. "Sorry. Guess I was daydreaming."

John smiled. "Claudia does that a lot. Must be a female thing."

"Excuse me?" Claudia said, jabbing him in the arm with her finger. "That sounds like a sexist remark."

"Sexist? Did that sound sexist to you?" John asked Lorna with an innocent look.

Lorna grinned. Their playful teasing always amused her. "Well, since you asked..."

"Don't tell me you *agree* with her?" he said.

In answer, Lorna only laughed.

"What'd you think about last night?" Claudia said, ignoring John, who was shaking his head in feigned disbelief.

"Except for seeing Nick DeSanto, it was a pretty nice evening," Lorna said.

Claudia made a face. "Did you see that babe he was with?"

"I noticed her," John said.

Claudia rolled her eyes. "I'm sure you did. I'm sure every man in the place did. How could they help it?" Turning back to Lorna, she said, "Nick DeSanto sure wasn't very friendly."

"Well, we didn't exactly act overjoyed to see *him*." As soon as the words were out of her mouth, Lorna wondered why she'd defended him.

"No, I guess not." Brightening, Claudia said, "Enough about him. What'd you think of Jonah?"

"He's nice."

"Just nice?"

"He liked *you* a lot," John said, chiming in. He reached for a roll and broke it in two.

Lorna sighed. "Look. The thing is, he's too young for me."

"He's only two years younger than you are," John pointed out.

"And he's really cute," Claudia added.

Lorna shrugged.

"He told me he'd like to see you again," John said.

"Please don't encourage him to ask me out. I'm sorry, but he's just not my type."

Now it was Claudia's turn to sigh. "Lorna…"

Lorna swung her gaze to her sister. "I mean it. If he *does* call me, I'm just going to make an excuse."

"We're only trying to help. Since you're new in town and all."

"I know you are, but I don't need help."

After an awkward moment of silence, John reached over and squeezed her shoulder. "You're right. You don't. We should butt out."

Claudia fell silent after that, and Lorna felt bad.

She knew her sister only wanted her to be happy. But Lorna had to find happiness in her own way. Besides, she wasn't *unhappy.* She simply hoped for a future that would yield something more.

Once again, her thoughts turned to Coach. Maybe she *was* being too cautious. Who knew? He could turn out to be perfect for her. *Go ahead. Take another chance.*

"You're daydreaming again," Claudia chided.

Lorna determinedly cleared her mind and for the rest of their time together, concentrated on participating in the conversation.

After brunch, Lorna said goodbye to Claudia and John—who were going to a photography exhibit John wanted to see—and headed for the Galleria, where she spent a pleasant couple of hours shopping. She hit Nordstrom's, Neiman Marcus, the new Foley's and several of the smaller boutiques. She even managed to find a few Christmas presents, although the holiday wasn't for months. She was particularly pleased with the gorgeous James Avery crosses she bought for her nieces. She was sure the girls would love them. In a spurt of inspiration, she bought two extra crosses—one for Emily when she was old enough to wear it, and one for Claudia's baby, in case she had a girl. And if she didn't have a girl this time, she might in the future.

Or I might, Lorna thought. Just the thought gave her goosebumps. *A little girl of my own...* Lorna already knew that if she was ever blessed with a daughter, she would name her Diana after her great-great-grandmother Diana Morgan, who had been married to Jeremiah Morgan. Sometimes Lorna dreamed about her baby, imagining she'd even look like her ancestor, who'd had dark hair and eyes and had been a great beauty in her day.

At Neiman Marcus, Lorna bought a wonderful deep purple brocade jacket that would look beautiful on her grandmother and also found a wispy gold chiffon scarf for her mother. All in all, a satisfying afternoon.

After leaving the Galleria, she stopped at the supermarket and stocked up on groceries, then headed home.

By the time she'd put her groceries away, nuked and eaten some frozen lasagna, and finished reading the newspaper, it was nearly eight o'clock and time to log on to Jamboree. She was really looking forward to playing against and talking to Coach again.

She logged on and entered the games area. She hadn't been listed for more than a couple of seconds when Coach sent her an invitation to join him.

Glad you made it. Ready to lose? he wrote in the chat box.

She grinned. Them's fightin' words, mister.

Put on your gloves, then.

He had the first turn and, as luck would have it, made a seven-letter word—*Sponges*—which gained him not only the value of the letters times two but a thirty-five-point bonus.

See? he wrote. Told you I was going to skunk you.

Lorna laughed. You may have to eat those words, you know. She looked at her letters: *X, R, I, I, M, A, H.* Smiling, she played off his *E,* making the word *Mixer.* It seemed only fitting since sponge mixers played an important part in the commercial baking business.

His next word was *Raisin,* which he played off the *R* in *Mixer.* Lorna shook her head. It was almost as if he'd understood the significance of the first two words in her life and was responding with one of the types of breads Hathaway was famous for. If she'd had the right combination of letters, she would have made the word *Bread,* but she didn't. Besides, it would only have been a private joke and would mean nothing to Coach.

They played quickly after that, neither one taking very long to decide on a word, and less than thirty minutes later, as Coach had predicted, he came out the victor, but she beat him soundly in the next game.

Told you so, he typed. But then I'm not the type to gloat.

You're not?, she responded, then why are you mentioning your win? Don't know about you, but I call that gloating.

You're right, he wrote back, I should just be happy I'm smarter than you are without rubbing it in.

Lorna laughed out loud. Oh, boy, those are really fightin' words.

They played four games in all, and when they were finished, they'd split the wins, two and two.

Another? he wrote.

She looked at the clock. I'd better not. I didn't tell you, but I'm starting a new job tomorrow and I want to get a good night's sleep.

A new job at another company? he typed.

No, not another company, she wrote back. A new position.

So you got a promotion? Good for you, he answered.

Lorna didn't want to lie. But how could she respond to his question truthfully without revealing more than she was ready to reveal? No, not a promotion exactly. Just something different.

Oh? he wrote. But I thought you really liked your job.

Lorna thought for a minute, then wrote, I just felt like I wanted a change.

It took him a few seconds to reply. I can understand that. We all need a change sometimes. In fact, I might be in for a big change myself.

Now it was her turn to say, Oh?

By now he had switched to instant messaging, writing, I think the PTB might be trying to run me off.

PTB? Lorna typed.

Powers That Be, he answered.

That doesn't sound good, she wrote. As she had many times before, she wondered exactly what it was that Coach did. Yet she hesitated to ask him. After all, if he wanted her to know, he'd tell her. Just as if she wanted *him* to know, she'd be more specific about *her* job.

No, it's not, he replied.

So what are you going to do about it?

I don't know yet. Guess I'll just play it by ear. See how things go, then figure out my game plan.

That's smart, because you could be wrong.

Yeah, that's always possible, but I don't think so.

Well, good luck, she wrote.

Yeah, you, too. So do you think you'll play Word-Maker again tomorrow night?

Probably, she replied.

I may have to stay at work late, but if not, I'll be here. I'll be looking forward to hearing about your first day at your new job.

They said goodbye, then Lorna fed Buttercup, fixed the coffeepot for the morning and prepared for bed. But once there, she couldn't fall asleep. Her mind refused to shut down. She kept thinking about the next day and what might be in store for her, both with the job itself and her uneasy relationship with Nick DeSanto. Then she thought about Coach and *their* relationship and whether she should trust her instincts about him.

But most of all, she thought about the future and whether this move to Houston would bring about the changes she hoped for.

On Monday, Nick arrived at the plant before seven, determined to beat Lorna there. Although the office itself didn't open until eight, he figured she'd show up early. Sure enough, at seven-thirty, Henry, the security guard who manned the main entrance, passed her through.

If she was surprised to see Nick already there, she hid it well. "Good morning," she said.

"Good morning." She sure looked different than the way she'd looked Saturday night. Today her outfit was all business—dark blue tailored slacks and a matching jacket over a conservative white blouse. If they'd been on halfway friendly terms, he probably would have said something to that effect. "Before we get started, let's go up to my office and go over a few things, okay?"

"Sure."

When they reached the office level, Nick stopped at the doorway to the kitchen. "Want some coffee? I'm going to grab a quick cup."

"I've already had my cup for the day, but thanks."

"Doughnuts? Fresh baked right here during the night."

She shook her head. "Bad enough I'll be smelling them all day long."

"Is there a woman alive who isn't watching her weight?" Nick said. He poured fresh coffee into his mug.

"It's not that. I just eat too many sweets. A hazard of the business, I'm afraid."

Nick mentally rolled his eyes. It was hard for him to reconcile today's rigid demeanor with the woman he'd watched on the dance floor Saturday night. If he hadn't seen her with his own eyes, he wouldn't have believed they were one and the same person.

Once they were settled in his office, he handed her a stack of reports and a disk that contained all the information she'd need to access the financial records and any other pertinent data from their computer system. While they were going over the current inventory, he heard rustling noises in the outer office and knew Karen was setting up for the day. A few minutes later, she knocked on his door, then opened it.

"Nick," she began, then stopped. "Oh, Miss Hathaway, I didn't know you were here. I was just going to tell Nick that your temp has arrived."

Lorna started to rise.

"Why not have Karen show her the ropes first?" he suggested. "I'm sure the temp's got paperwork to fill out, and Karen can brief her on our computer system and where things are located."

"Maybe Karen could show *both* of us these things at the same time," Lorna said.

"Sure. I don't mind," Karen said.

Nick hated to admit it, but Lorna's willingness to expose her ignorance in front of the temp produced another bout of grudging admiration. "Great. I'll leave you to it. And Karen?"

"Yes?"

"Shut the door on your way out."

After they were gone, Nick leaned back in his chair and wondered if he'd misjudged Lorna. Maybe she *hadn't* come to spy on him. He had to admit she wasn't throwing her weight around or acting like she owned the place, even if she did. He guessed only time would tell. It could be she was just biding her time before lowering the boom.

Until then, he decided, he would play if safe and never let his guard down.

* * *

By the time the day was over, Lorna was exhausted. She'd never imagined there would be so much for her to learn. Thank goodness Karen was so knowledgeable and didn't seem to mind spending a good portion of her day showing Lorna, never mind the temp, the ropes.

In fact, the temp—whose name was Marilyn— was excellent. A no-nonsense type with terrific skills, she settled in as if she'd been there forever. By mid-afternoon, Lorna was ready to offer Marilyn the secretarial position on a permanent basis. Prudently, she decided to wait another day or two, just to make sure they were compatible.

Toward the end of the day, Phyllis McIntyre, the bookkeeper, came by to introduce herself. An elfin woman with short black hair and shrewd eyes behind bifocals, she impressed Lorna immediately.

"If you'd rather I work here in the plant," she said, "I'd be happy to."

"You don't *like* telecommuting?" Lorna said.

"Oh, no, I *love* it, but after all, you're the boss, and if you'd prefer me to be here, well, then I'll come in."

Her offer impressed Lorna, too. Most employees with the kind of deal Phyllis had would be loath to give it up. "I don't have a problem with you working from home."

After discussing Phyllis's schedule and responsibilities, Lorna knew they were on their way to a solid working relationship.

Another plus during the day was how little she saw of Nick. If every day was like this one, she had nothing to worry about.

That evening, after a quick pick-me-up dinner of tomato soup and a grilled cheese sandwich, Lorna decided to take a bath and get comfortable before going online to Jamboree.

At 7:45 p.m., feeling much better, she logged on to her computer so she could check her e-mail before heading over to the games server. She smiled when she saw an e-mail from Coach in her inbox.

FROM: Coach1012@bayoucity.net
TO: SweetStuff@jamboree.net
DATE: September 1
SUBJECT: Change of Plans
Dear Sweet Stuff, I'm sorry, but I can't play tonight. Something's come up and I had to go back to work. I'll probably be here half the night. Whenever I get a break, I'll check my e-mail, though. I'm really curious about how your first day at your new job went. Things were really interesting here. One of these days I'll tell you all about it. Anyway, right now I've got to go, but I hope to hear from you later.

Lorna was disappointed, but she had a good book to read. Maybe she'd just climb into bed and read until she got sleepy. First, though, she'd answer his post.

FROM: SweetStuff@jamboree.net
TO: Coach1012@bayoucity.net
DATE: September 1
SUBJECT: Re: Change of Plans
I'm sorry, too. I was feeling lucky and planned to give you a good beating tonight. LOL. Anyway, hope the problem at work isn't too serious and that you get home at a decent hour.

You asked about my day. It went well, much better than I expected it to. Sometime I'll tell you all about my job, too. In fact, I may be in need of advice, and someone impartial could probably give me better suggestions than anyone in my family or any of my friends, who are mostly female. In this case, I think a man's opinion is called for. The thing is, I'm working with a man I don't much like, and I don't think he likes me. I could really use some pointers on how to handle him, although I have to be honest and say he was actually quite decent today.

Okay, enough about that. Good luck with the problem at work, and let me know if you plan to be online tomorrow night.

Lorna signed the e-mail and sent it. Stretching, she began to log off. Just as she did, Buttercup, who had been twining herself around Lorna's legs and making "feed me" noises, jumped up onto Lorna's desk and knocked her glass of water over.

Lorna let out a yelp and grabbed for it, but she wasn't quick enough. Thank goodness it was only about a third full, and none of it fell onto her keyboard.

In the time it took to clean up the desk and feed Buttercup, another e-mail from Coach arrived.

FROM: Coach1012@bayoucity.net
TO: SweetStuff@jamboree.net
DATE: September 1
SUBJECT: Re: Re: Change of Plans
Glad to hear you had a good day at work. And I'd be happy to see if I can help if you want to tell me about this guy who's giving you trouble.

About tomorrow night—I probably won't be online. My folks will be happily married forty-six years tomorrow, and my sister is having everyone over for dinner. It'll probably be late by the time I get home.

How about Wednesday night?

Lorna felt a pang as she read about his parents. Her father had died the previous year. Even if he hadn't, her parents' marriage was not a happy one.

Wouldn't it be wonderful to be able to say your parents had been happily married that long? Coach was lucky. She wondered if he knew that. Maybe someday—if they ever met in person—she would tell him so.

Quickly, hoping she'd catch him before he logged off, she zapped an e-mail to him saying she had nothing planned for Wednesday night and would be online by eight and would love to talk to him.

Then she shut down her computer and headed to bed.

Nick hoped the problem with the cooler wasn't going to be chronic, but he didn't have a good feeling about it. This was the second time in less than three days that it had broken down and caused them to lose precious hours. Not to mention money.

He swore. He would have to have that talk with Bryce sooner rather than later. He knew Bryce would be reasonable, but he wouldn't be happy. The Houston plant was already over its equipment budget for the year. And considering they would also soon need to spend big bucks on expansion....

But it couldn't be helped. Jim Hennessey said the problem with the cooler was it was simply worn out. You couldn't use a piece of equipment forever.

It was after midnight before they finally got it

running again and, after assuring himself the night crew didn't need him to stay, Nick headed on home.

Although he was tired and more than ready for bed, Maggie needed attention. Once he'd seen to her, he decided he might as well check his e-mail before hitting the sack. He knew his brothers would tease him mercilessly if they knew he had struck up a friendship with a woman online—one that had come to mean a lot to him.

He grinned when a message from her down-loaded. He clicked it open and read.

FROM: SweetStuff@jamboree.net
TO: Coach1012@bayoucity.net
DATE: September 1
SUBJECT: Re: Re: Re: Change of Plans
Thanks for saying you're willing to listen to my problem with the guy at work. I'd love to talk to you about it. And Wednesday night at eight is great. See you then!

He was still grinning twenty minutes later when he climbed into bed and Maggie hopped up beside him. Maybe it was time for him to meet Sweet Stuff. He'd hesitated suggesting it before because he knew she was leery of a face-to-face meeting. Hell, he didn't blame her. There were a lot of slick con men out there. She had no way of knowing he wasn't one of them.

At first, he'd been leery, too, and glad when she'd suggested not exchanging identifying information. But he no longer felt that way. He could be kidding himself, believing what he wanted to be true rather than what was true, but he didn't think so.

Sweet Stuff was on the up-and-up—a genuinely nice woman who was down to earth, smart and funny, the kind of woman both his sister and his mother would approve of. He'd bet money on it. Now if she was sexy and attractive, too, who knew what might come of this?

He scratched Maggie's head, and she sighed, settling closer to him. "Whatta you think, Maggie? Think I ought to suggest meeting her?"

The dog made a contented sound deep in her throat.

"Okay, but be warned. If this works out the way I hope it will, someone else may be replacing you in this bed!"

Chapter Four

On the way to work Wednesday morning, Lorna decided she would spend the day getting to know the employees and familiarizing herself with the step-by-step process in the production of baked goods for the Houston market. That was the biggest difference between the Morgan Creek plant and the Houston plant. Morgan Creek's facility produced baked goods for national distribution, whereas the Houston facility produced only for the local area.

Since there was no one else to do it, Lorna would be in charge of conducting tours in Houston, making it doubly important for her to have a complete understanding of the hows and whys of what took place throughout the production process.

But the main reason—even if she'd barely admitted it to herself—that she wanted to know as much as possible about the Houston plant was so she would never again be caught off guard by Nick DeSanto.

Because she expected to spend most of the day on the plant floor, where it was always very warm and humid, she'd dressed accordingly in lightweight khaki pants, tennis shoes and a cotton T-shirt.

She didn't see Nick in his office when she passed by, although Karen was already typing away at her computer. Lorna poked her head in the door. "Good morning."

Karen looked up. "Good morning, Miss Hathaway."

"Nick around?"

Karen shook her head. "He was here until after midnight last night so he hasn't gotten in yet. The cooler broke down again."

Lorna frowned. "Again?" She didn't like the sound of that. The cooler was an essential piece of equipment and caused more problems when it was down than any other machine on the line. None of the bread or other baked goods could be packaged until they were cooled, so everything came to a standstill when they had cooler problems. "Well, when he shows up, tell him if he wants me, I'll be down on the plant floor most of the day."

"Oh. Okay." She hesitated a moment. "What about Marilyn?"

"What about her?" Lorna heard the defensive tone in her voice and inwardly berated herself for reading criticism into Karen's question, which had probably been perfectly innocent.

"Do you want me to help her out if she has any questions?"

Lorna relaxed. "If you wouldn't mind. However, I do think she's got enough to keep her busy until lunch. There were stacks of purchase orders that needed inputting, plus the end-of-the-month report."

Karen nodded, and before Lorna was out the door, her red head was already bent back over her keyboard. Lorna wondered if Nick knew how lucky he was to have such a conscientious secretary who worked hard whether he was around to see her or not.

As Lorna made her way downstairs, she decided she'd have a look at the problematic cooler before doing anything else. She grabbed a hairnet from the bin at the bottom of the stairs and put it on. She thought about removing her watch and rings—no one was allowed to wear any kind of jewelry when around the equipment—but the watch was the strap-on kind and there was no danger it would fall off, and the rings were tight and difficult to remove, so *they* certainly wouldn't be falling off. Anyway, she wouldn't be bending over any of the equipment. She would just be observing.

Walking carefully—the plant floor could be slippery from excess oil or flour—she headed straight for the cooling area. Raisin bread was currently moving along the line, and the smell of the freshly baked loaves made Lorna's mouth water, even though she'd had breakfast. Cal Lopez, the production manager whom Lorna had met previously, stood watching the workers as they manned the line leading to the cooler.

She stood back and watched, too. It always fascinated her to see how the de-panner suctioned the bread out of the loaf pans in preparation for sending them into the cooler where, when they reached the proper temperature, they would then move along the line to the metal detector.

Lorna had always gotten a kick out of how outsiders' eyes widened at the realization that the bread they bought in stores had to go through a metal detector before it could be bagged and sold. But that was a necessary step to avoid serious and costly problems later. The last thing Hathaway or any other reputable baker wanted was for someone to choke on a piece of metal that might have loosened or broken off of the equipment during the baking process and subsequently fallen into the batter.

Cal Lopez turned to say something to one of the workers and saw Lorna. Walking over to her, he said, "Did you want to talk to me?" He had to raise his voice to be heard over the noise.

Lorna smiled and shook her head. "No. I just wanted to observe for a while. Get acquainted with the workers and the way you do things here."

He nodded, but there was a look in his dark eyes that told Lorna he wasn't sure he believed her. She was beginning to realize it might take awhile before the people here would entirely trust her. She was also beginning to realize she'd been naive to think she could just come to Houston and step into this job and have it be smooth sailing from then on.

She watched awhile longer and was just turning to go to another station when she saw Nick approaching. Although she still didn't particularly like him, she had to admit she could see why most women did. He was an attractive man—not conventionally handsome—but extremely sexy with his thick, dark hair, melted chocolate eyes and athletic body. Although he hadn't turned it her way very often, he also had an amazing smile. But mostly he had this air about him, one that said he was strong and decisive. Those traits would be appealing to most women. Actually, in another man, they would be appealing to Lorna, too. After all, what woman *wouldn't* want a man who could make a decision and who didn't need constant ego stroking?

The way he walked reminded her of a big jungle cat. It was a "watch out, here I come" walk, one that drew your attention. Maybe that—his complete assurance of his self-worth—was what set Lorna's teeth on edge, even as she could objectively appreciate his attributes. Did the man never doubt he might not be as great as he thought he was?

He nodded to her, then walked over to Cal. "How behind are we?"

Cal shook his head. "We'll have to short some of our accounts, but it's not too bad."

When Nick didn't say anything, Lorna walked over and joined the two men. "Isn't this the second time we've had a cooler breakdown in just a few days?"

"Yes," Nick answered.

"What's the problem?"

"The cooler is wearing out, Miss Hathaway," Cal said. "We've been babying it along, but it looks like it's going to have to be replaced sooner than we'd figured."

Nick didn't say anything, just rubbed his jaw and watched the continual flow of bread on the line.

"I know that'll play hell with the bottom line and the brass probably won't be hap—" Cal broke off, darting a glance at Lorna.

The brass.

He meant Bryce and had obviously momentarily forgotten Bryce's sister was standing next to him. Well, Cal was right. Bryce *wouldn't* be happy about having to replace a piece of equipment that should have lasted several more years, but he would do it because there was no other choice. After all, they would be out a lot more money if their accounts started cancelling orders because of chronic production problems.

Turning to Nick, she said, "I'll give Bryce a call and discuss it with him."

For a moment, he said nothing. Then to Cal, he said, "We'll talk later." He swung his gaze to her. "Let's go up to my office."

As they walked away, Lorna knew just by the set of his jaw that he was furious and guessed she shouldn't have suggested calling Bryce. She gave a mental sigh. No matter what she did, she couldn't seem to win with Nick.

Karen gave them a curious glance when they walked in. "No calls, Karen," Nick said. He motioned to Lorna to precede him. Once they were inside his office, he shut the door.

His dark eyes were hard. "Don't ever do that again."

"Look, I was only trying to help and—"

"I don't need your help to do my job. I especially don't need your interference when it comes to dealing with the head office. Is that understood?"

Now Lorna was getting mad. Why was he making such a big deal out of an innocent remark? "Fine," she bit off. "But I have a stake in this business, too, you know."

"Let's get something crystal clear, *Miss Hathaway.* Your job here includes public relations, the purchasing of supplies and the supervision of all the bookkeeping, including payroll, accounts receivable and accounts payable. It does *not* include a voice in sales, marketing strategy, or plant management of any kind. That's *my* job. And for your information, I've already called your brother and I'm going to Morgan Creek to talk to him next week."

Lorna practically bit her tongue off to keep from saying something she'd be sorry for later. Although it galled her to admit it, down deep, she knew he was right. She had been out of line to say she would call Bryce. And she'd compounded her error by making the statement in front of Cal Lopez. "I'm sorry. You're right. It won't happen again."

She turned to leave.

"And Lorna?"

"Yes?" She stopped but didn't turn around.

"I'd appreciate it if you would remove your jewelry before going down to the floor. It sets a bad example to the employees when the management doesn't follow the rules."

Thoroughly embarrassed now, Lorna wished she could crawl back into bed and start the day over. She finally turned and met his gaze levelly. "That won't happen again, either."

"Good."

As Lorna made her way back downstairs, she promised herself that even if it killed her, this morning's dressing-down at the hands of Nick DeSanto would be the last one she'd ever receive.

Do you think we should meet?

Lorna blinked. Just the thought of coming face to face with Coach made her heart beat faster. After a moment, she wrote: Meet?

Yeah, meet, he answered back.

Lorna bit her lip. Finally she wrote, I don't know. Do you think we should meet? She was stalling for time. It was Wednesday night, and she and Coach had just finished playing three games of WordMaker, and they were now sending instant messages.

It took a few seconds for him to type his reply. Yeah, I've been thinking maybe it's time.

Lorna wasn't sure what to say. While she was still considering her answer, he sent another message.

I'm going to be in your area next week.

Lorna stared at his message. She'd expected something like this to happen eventually. She just hadn't expected it to happen so soon. She wished she knew what to do.

So I thought maybe we could get together for dinner one night, he wrote.

She sighed. She knew the time had come to tell

Coach about her move to Houston. He'd forced her hand, so she couldn't put it off any longer.

Well, she wrote, the thing is, I moved awhile back, so I'm no longer living in the Austin area.

For a few moments, nothing happened.

You moved? he finally wrote.

She knew by the length of time it had taken him to answer that he was dumbfounded. Yes.

Why didn't you tell me?

I wanted to wait awhile.

Wait? Why? Where are you living now?

Lorna wondered what he'd think when he read her answer. She typed: I'm in Houston.

Houston!

Yes.

Are you working in Houston?

Yes. Are you mad at me for not telling you? She hoped not. She valued their friendship, and she didn't want anything to spoil it.

I'm not mad, he wrote, I'm just wondering why you didn't want to tell me.

Once more Lorna sighed. She thought about fudging a bit, then decided the truth was always best. Because I knew you'd want to meet, and I wasn't ready.

Again it took him a long moment to reply. And are you ready now?

Lorna stared at the screen. Was she? She wanted to meet Coach and yet she didn't want to meet him. What if he was disappointed in her? What if she was disappointed in *him?* Their friendship would be ruined.

I don't know, she wrote.

Are you afraid?

She nodded, then realized how ridiculous that was. He couldn't see her. Yes, I guess I am. What if we don't like each other?

We'll like each other. This was followed by a smiley face icon.

She grinned. You sound so confident.

Hey, I'm a guy. It's part of guy rules that you always sound confident, whether you are or not.

Now Lorna laughed. She did like him so much! Come on, he wrote. My mother always says nothing ventured, nothing gained.

She smiled. I wish I had a mother who said things like that.

Do you want mine? he wrote back. Only kidding. She's great. I wouldn't trade her.

Lorna wished she could say the same. Oh, she loved her mother, but she'd never felt close to her.

Well? he wrote. What's it going to be? Are we going to meet?

Lorna took a deep breath. Okay, she said, Let's meet. After sending the message, her heart was beating as fast as if she'd just taken a leap off a cliff. And in some ways, she *had* taken a big leap, hadn't she? For too long she'd kept her heart safe by staying in her own little fenced-in world, but with a few key strokes, she had agreed to come out into unknown, and possibly dangerous, territory.

If you could see me now, you'd see the big smile on my face, he wrote.

Now that she'd taken the plunge, she couldn't stop smiling herself. When shall we meet? she wrote.

How about Saturday afternoon?

Okay. Where?

You pick the place.

Lorna thought hard. She remembered all the things she'd read about meeting men online, how you needed to be very careful. Even though she was ninety-nine percent sure Coach was a good guy and she had nothing to fear from him, she knew she still shouldn't take any chances. She wanted a public place, one where there would be lots of people.

How about the skating rink at the Galleria? she suggested.

Okay. What time?

Lorna didn't want to suggest a time too near lunch because if she didn't like him, she didn't want to be stuck eating with him. How about two o'clock?

Okay, that's good. What level?

Lorna thought for a moment. Second level.

How will I know you?

She smiled. I'm a tall blonde and I'll be wearing a red dress... Her smile widened. And carrying a bag of Hathaway chocolate-chip cookies.

It took a few seconds for him to answer. How'd you know they're my favorite?

Aren't they everyone's?

After telling her he had dark hair and would be dressed in black jeans and a black T-shirt, they signed off.

It took Lorna a long time to fall asleep that night. She kept thinking about finally meeting Coach. What would he be like? What if he was ugly? Would it matter to her? No, she decided, not if he was as nice and funny in person as he was online. His looks wouldn't be important. But even as she told herself this, she hoped he would be attractive. Not drop-dead handsome or anything. Just attractive, with a nice smile.

Even as she cautioned herself not to expect too much, because she was bound to be disappointed, she couldn't banish the flutter of excitement in the pit of her stomach.

Maybe Saturday would be the beginning of a wonderful new chapter in her life.

"You're doing *what?*"

Lorna grinned sheepishly. It was Thursday night and the sisters were having dinner together. Lorna had just told Claudia about Coach. "Do you think I'm crazy?"

"No, it's just that doing something like this is so *unlike* you, Lorna. You're not the adventurous type. You're not even *spontaneous.*"

"Gee, thanks."

"Oh, come on, I didn't mean it that way."

Lorna picked at the remains of her salad. "I know exactly how you meant it."

"C'mon, Lorna…"

"Listen, I know I'm too staid and cautious. You don't have to rub it in."

"You're not staid. You're…sensible."

"Maybe I'm tired of being sensible."

"There's nothing wrong with being sensible."

"Make up your mind, will you?"

Claudia laughed. "Actually, I'm glad you're going to meet him, but I'm even happier you picked such a public place. Just don't go anywhere with him until you're absolutely sure he's okay."

"I won't."

"Promise."

Lorna rolled her eyes. "I promise."

"And also promise me you'll call me if there's anything at all that makes you nervous. In fact, do you want John and me to be somewhere close by? We could station ourselves on the first level. That way, if anything bothers you, we could be up there in a flash."

"I don't think that's necessary. What could happen to me at the Galleria? It's not like I'm going to meet him in a dark parking garage or anything."

"Well, okay. If you're sure…"

They stopped talking when their waiter approached

with their entrées—poached salmon for Claudia, crab cakes for Lorna.

Once he was gone, Claudia leaned forward eagerly. "Okay, now tell me everything. Start from the beginning. Just when did you first meet this guy?"

So while they ate, Lorna gave Claudia a blow-by-blow account of her relationship with Coach. When she'd finished, Claudia sighed, saying, "This is very romantic, you know."

"You're a big help."

"What do you mean? It *is* romantic."

"Look, I'm trying not to get my hopes up too high, okay?"

"I think it's too late for that."

Lorna made a face. "Yeah, I'm afraid you're right."

"So what'll you do if he's really ugly? You know, so ugly you can't even look at him?" Claudia started mugging, crossing her eyes and making monster noises.

"Claudia!" Lorna started to laugh. Soon they were both giggling like teenagers.

"He doesn't have to be handsome," Lorna said when they had settled down.

"Oh, I know, but it wouldn't hurt."

"No."

"You do want him to be tall, though," Claudia said.

Lorna nodded. She was five foot ten, and although she knew there were lots of tall women who didn't seem to mind shorter men—take Nicole Kidman and Tom Cruise, for example—although look how that turned out!—Lorna didn't like towering over a man, and even though she knew it was shallow of her, she didn't relish spending the rest of her life wearing flat shoes, either.

"So what are you going to wear?" Claudia asked.

"My red sleeveless dress and those new red sandals I bought." Lorna smiled. "The lady in red. I should be pretty easy to spot."

"I want you to call me *immediately* afterwards. Immediately."

"I will."

"Have you told Chloe about this?"

Lorna shook her head. Chloe was their older sister. She was married and lived in Austin with her advertising manager husband and their almost-seventeen-year-old daughter. "She's gotten pretty stodgy, all Junior League and everything. I was afraid she'd start lecturing me."

Claudia grimaced. "Yeah, she gets more like Mother every year."

"You noticed that, too?"

"How could I not? I mean, any day I expect her to start putting her hair in a chignon and wearing Barbara Bush pearls." Claudia shuddered. "God, I hope I never get like that."

Lorna, thinking of Claudia's navel ring, started to

laugh. "I don't think there's much danger of that happening."

They talked awhile more, then paid their bill and left the restaurant. After hugging goodbye, they entered their respective vehicles and headed home.

As Lorna started her car, she breathed a silent prayer that she was not also headed straight for heartbreak by agreeing to meet Coach.

Chapter Five

Lorna woke up at six on Saturday, even though it was her one day to sleep in, and normally she relished it. But knowing she was going to meet Coach that afternoon, she was too nervous and excited to sleep.

All morning, the meeting was all she could think about. She still could hardly believe she was going. The closest she had ever come to being this daring was when she was in college and had gone skinny-dipping during a fraternity party. That escapade she'd put down to being nineteen and immature.

But this was fifteen years later. Now she was a thirty-four-year-old woman with a master's degree, a responsible job and a failed marriage. She was through with risky business.

So what am I doing? Why don't I do what I said I'd do and join a church and meet people the safe, old-fashioned way?

Claudia hadn't thought Lorna was being irresponsible, but Claudia had always been more of a free spirit than her sisters. What would Amy say? Lorna wondered. Amy was even more down-to-earth than Lorna, yet she wasn't stodgy like Chloe. On impulse, Lorna picked up her cell phone and punched in the speed-dial code for her brother's house.

"Oh, good," she said when Amy answered. "You're home."

"Hi, Lorna. Yes, we're here. Later we're driving into Austin to do some shopping and then meeting Chloe and Greg for dinner, but that's not until about one."

Amy chattered on for a while, updating Lorna on the girls. Then she wanted to know about Lorna's job. When they'd exhausted that topic, Lorna finally had a chance to introduce the subject of Coach and their impending meeting.

"So what do you think?" she said when she'd finished.

"You like this guy, don't you?"

"Yes," Lorna admitted.

"Then I think you're doing the right thing. And Lorna?"

"Yes?"

"I want to hear every single detail. Darn. I wish I was going to be home later. Well, tomorrow then. I'll call you when we get back from church, okay?"

"Okay."

"This is *so* exciting."

Lorna grinned. "Yes."

"Oh, Lorna, I hope he's all you want him to be."

"Me, too," Lorna said fervently. *Me, too.*

Later, as Lorna showered and got ready for the big meeting, she wondered why she'd felt the need for so much reassurance. Maybe she ought to sign up for some classes on decision-making. Then she chuckled. Or maybe she just needed a shrink.

By twelve-thirty she was ready and too fidgety to sit around, so she headed off to the Galleria, stopping at a Hathaway Sweet Shop on the way to purchase the cookies.

Her heart was beating fast as she entered the Galleria parking garage. Because it was way too early to go to the agreed-upon meeting place, she decided she would check out the sales at Nordstrom.

She found nothing she really wanted to buy, so at ten minutes before two, she walked to the escalator bank closest to the ice-skating rink.

A very large man entered the escalator ahead of her, blocking her view as they rode slowly to the second level. Butterflies churned in Lorna's stomach.

Just before stepping off, she whispered a little prayer that the meeting would go well and that Coach would be everything she'd hoped he would be.

Then, taking a deep breath, she walked purposefully toward the railing overlooking the rink.

Nick arrived at the Galleria at one-thirty. As he walked from the parking garage into the main part of Galleria I, he cautioned himself once again not to expect too much. The woman he knew as Sweet Stuff might seem great online, but she could turn out to be a real bitch in person.

He *had* taken one precaution, just in case. He wasn't wearing black, even though he'd told her he would be. Instead, he'd put on faded blue jeans and a dark blue shirt. That way he figured he could go up to the second level, park himself somewhere unobtrusive, and get a look at her before she saw him.

And if I don't like her, I can leave....

No.

He wouldn't do that. That would be the action of a jerk. He just wanted a heads-up, so that if she disappointed him, he wouldn't show it. He'd have a few minutes to prepare before actually approaching her.

Because it was still too early to go to the second level, he stayed on the main floor. Standing at the rail of the ice-skating rink, he idly watched the skaters.

One girl, obviously not simply a weekend skater, practiced jumps in the center of the rink. Nick smiled. She was good. He continued to watch another ten minutes or so, then headed for the escalator.

On the second level, he found a good spot alongside a kiosk at the western end of the rink. Pretending to be looking at a jewelry display, he surreptitiously scanned the railing around the rink to see if Sweet Stuff had arrived yet. There was no woman in a red dress anywhere in sight.

For the next five minutes, he kept a sharp eye on both the escalator and the steps as well as periodically glancing around to see if a woman in a red dress walked out of one of the shops.

Suddenly he saw a flash of red on the escalator coming from the first level. He couldn't tell if the red belonged to a woman or a man because an enormous man hid the person from view. Finally the man reached the top and moved out of the way.

Nick blinked.

What?

He looked again.

What the hell was *she* doing here?

For coming off the escalator was none other than Lorna Hathaway. Nick couldn't believe it. Lorna Hathaway! Stunned, he stared at her, watching as she walked past the kiosk and toward the railing that overlooked the rink. She stopped, then slowly looked around. He ducked back so she wouldn't see him, then cautiously looked out again.

It was unbelievable, but no matter how many times he blinked, the same image remained. Lorna Hathaway was there wearing a red dress and carrying a bag of Hathaway cookies.

Was it a coincidence?

No. It couldn't be.

The truth was undeniable.

Lorna Hathaway was Sweet Stuff. Lorna Hathaway was his online friend, the one he'd been writing to and confiding in for months. The same Lorna Hathaway who knew his deepest fears and secret thoughts. The same Lorna Hathaway who had made no secret of her dislike for him. And the very same Lorna Hathaway who was miles and miles out of his league.

He was so stunned that for a few moments, he remained frozen, not knowing what to do. But as the reality of his discovery sank in, he knew he had to leave. There was no way he could talk to her or even let her see him.

His only choice was to go.

So while her back was turned, he quickly walked to the down escalator and got on. His heart was banging away in his chest as if someone had been chasing him, and his mind was whirling.

Lorna.

Sweet Stuff.

Lorna!

By now Nick was down on the first floor, walking fast toward the garage entrance. All he wanted was to get out of there. To go home and digest this staggering revelation.

He was halfway to his car before he'd calmed down enough to start to think about Lorna.

She would be standing there waiting. Waiting for someone who wouldn't show up.

He imagined how she would feel. The way she'd look at her watch. How she'd keep waiting, thinking maybe something had happened. How eventually she'd finally give up and realize he wasn't coming.

Or worse. She might think he *had* come, seen her, been disappointed and left without saying anything.

He stopped walking.

Damn.

He couldn't do it.

He could not leave her there.

He had to go back.

Swearing under his breath, he reversed course and half walked, half sprinted back to the entrance. Quickly, he made his way to the escalator. He wasn't quite sure what he'd say when he got up to the second level, but he'd think of something.

* * *

Lorna was beginning to feel anxious. It was ten minutes after two, and Coach still hadn't shown up. What if he'd had second thoughts? What if he wasn't coming? Surely he wouldn't do that to her. After all, he was the one who'd suggested meeting.

Maybe he'd had an accident!

Lorna bit her bottom lip. If something like that had happened, there would be no way he could tell her. After all, he didn't have a name or a phone number. All he had was her Jamboree e-mail address, which didn't identify her at all.

Maybe he'd just been caught in traffic. Sometimes traffic around the Galleria and the Loop was horrendous and lately, it had been impossible, what with all the highway construction going on. Who knows? He could have been coming from the opposite direction and run into road work or a wreck.

Trying to stay positive, she decided she would wait until two-thirty, and then if he still hadn't shown up, she would leave. Not sure if he would come up on the escalator or approach from the opposite direction, she scanned the area slowly, so her back was turned when a familiar voice said, "Well, if it isn't Lorna Hathaway."

She whirled around.

Nick DeSanto, looking extremely sexy in tight jeans and an open-necked blue shirt, stood there with an amused smile on his face.

"What are *you* doing here?" She wanted to kick herself for allowing him to see how he had disconcerted her. Why hadn't she just said something like "Oh, hi, Nick."

He shrugged. "I have some shopping to do. And you?" He glanced down at the bag of cookies in her hand. "I didn't know we had a Sweet Shop here."

"We don't," she snapped.

What was he *doing* here? Oh, God. This was the *last* thing she needed. She thought frantically. How could she get rid of him? She looked down at her watch. It was now a quarter after two. What if Coach *had* been delayed and finally showed up and found her talking to Nick? What would he think? She had to get Nick out of here. And fast.

"So where'd you buy the cookies, then?"

"I bought them a couple of blocks from here."

"I thought you said you try not to eat too many sweets."

Starting to feel desperate, she said, "Look, I'm meeting someone, so why don't you run along and do whatever it is you were going to do?"

He leaned against the railing. "I'm in no hurry. I don't mind waiting till your date shows up. It *is* a date, isn't it?"

"Yes, it's a date. But he'll be here any second, and, well, the truth is, I'd really prefer for you not to be here when he gets here."

"Why not?" Nick asked innocently.

Lorna was so frustrated, she could scream. She looked around. What if Coach was nearby right now? What would he *think?*

"What's wrong? Will your boyfriend be jealous if he sees me here?" Nick asked with that infuriating smile still on his face. "If he's that insecure, maybe you're better off without him."

Throwing caution out the door—after all, this was *not* a work situation and he had invaded *her* space—she said, "First of all, he's *not* my boyfriend. Secondly, if you were a gentleman, you'd go."

"Not your boyfriend, huh?"

Lorna glared at him.

"What time were you two supposed to meet?" Nick looked at his watch. "It's two-fifteen. Is he late?"

Lorna gritted her teeth. There was no way she'd admit Coach was late.

"He *is* late, isn't he? Tell you what. Why don't we wait a few more minutes, and if he doesn't show up, I'll take you for a cup of coffee or something. What about lunch? Have you eaten yet? There're some great restaurants here. My favorite is the Chinese place—"

"Thank you, no," she interrupted.

He looked at her for what seemed like a very long time. "You look very pretty today," he finally said.

And what was she supposed to answer to *that?*

"Too pretty to stand here and wait for a guy who can't even be on time."

Beyond caring what he thought, she said, "Why are you doing this?"

"Doing what?" He seemed honestly bewildered. "I'm just trying to be helpful."

"Would you please just *go?*"

His gaze locked with hers for a long moment. Then finally, he said, "Okay. Have it your way. I'm going." And with that, he gave her a salute, turned on his heel and walked off.

Lorna stared after him. This had not been her finest hour, she thought unhappily. She had been snotty to him, and what had he really done to deserve that kind of treatment? He'd just been in the wrong place at the wrong time. Other than that, he'd been friendly and complimentary.

Oh, Coach, where are you?

If he'd only come when he was supposed to, the episode with Nick wouldn't have happened. Sure, she might have still seen Nick, but she would have been with Coach. Everything would have ended up differently.

Alternately worrying about Coach and what might have happened to him and berating herself for the stupid way she'd acted with Nick, Lorna waited another twenty minutes. Finally, trying not to give way to an overwhelming disappointment, she had to admit that Coach wasn't coming.

On her way to the parking garage, she threw the bag of cookies into the trash.

Nick mentally kicked himself all the way home. He hadn't handled that episode with Lorna very well.

He was still having a hard time reconciling the fact that Lorna Hathaway had turned out to be the woman he knew as Sweet Stuff. Prickly Lorna, who didn't seem to have any sense of humor, was his amusing online buddy who always made him laugh. Haughty Lorna, who he'd always thought looked down her nose at him and everyone like him, was the compassionate and sensitive woman he'd gotten to know over the past seven months.

How was it possible she could be so different in person than she was in her e-mails and when she was playing WordMaker against him?

Obviously she wasn't.

Obviously it was only him, in the flesh, who brought out the worst in her.

Why hadn't he been nicer to her today?

Because, for some reason, she brings out the worst in you, too.

Nick knew he had to make a decision. Either he never again contacted Lorna as Sweet Stuff, letting her think whatever it was she wanted to think, or he had to figure out what to say to her to explain why he, as Coach, hadn't shown up today.

But the ultimate question was whether it was possible to ever tell her the truth.

"He didn't show *up?*"

Lorna heard the note of incredulity in Claudia's voice. "No."

"Oh, Lorna…"

Lorna sighed. "I know. It's really disappointing."

"I wonder why he didn't come."

"Something must have happened because he just doesn't seem like the kind of person who would do something like that."

"Maybe he had an accident."

"That's what I think."

"And, of course, he couldn't call you or anything because he doesn't know who you are."

"Right."

"Has he e-mailed you?"

"Not yet. But it's only three-thirty. I mean, if he had an accident, he might not be home yet."

"That's true."

For a moment, neither said anything.

"I'm sure that's what happened," Claudia said. "I'll bet you'll hear from him later today and he'll explain everything."

"I hope so."

But no matter how many times Lorna checked her e-mail during the rest of the day, there was nothing from Coach. Not at five. Not at six. And not at ten when she finally began to get ready for bed.

It took her a long time to fall asleep. Her mind went around and around. First she'd think about Coach and why she hadn't heard from him. And then she'd think about Nick and how he'd spoiled the day.

When she finally did fall asleep, she dreamed. It was one of those awful dreams where she was searching for something and couldn't find it. Sometimes Coach was there helping her, but he wasn't really Coach, he was Nick. She kept telling him to go away, but he wouldn't.

"But I can't find Coach if you're here," she cried.

"You could if you looked!" Nick said.

The next morning, she awakened with a headache. She felt exhausted from the dream and her fruitless and frustrating search.

Damn Nick DeSanto, she thought. *Not only do I have to put up with him at work, but now he's invaded my dreams.*

After washing her face, plugging in the coffee-maker, and downing some Advil, she headed straight for her computer. Impatiently, she waited for it to boot, then logged on to Jamboree and opened her mailbox there.

Thirteen messages downloaded.

Several wanted to sell her Viagra, several wanted to guide her to porn sites and several others were pushing cheap prescription medication. There was nothing from Coach.

Lorna's shoulders sagged.

Either he had been completely immobilized by some kind of awful accident and could not use a computer or he had come to the Galleria yesterday, seen her, decided he didn't like her and she would never hear from him again.

Surely not.

Surely Coach wouldn't do that to her.

She thought of all the confidences they'd exchanged. All the ways they'd revealed themselves to one another.

Coach *couldn't* do that to her.

Telling herself yesterday's nonmeeting wasn't the end of the world, that if she and Coach had been meant to meet, they would have, she began to get ready for church.

Chapter Six

Nick stood at the window in the room he used as his home office. He'd been watching the sunset, which had been spectacular tonight—vivid reds and golds gradually giving way to blue and lavender. That was one of the advantages of living where it was so flat—nothing obstructed the view of Texas's famously beautiful sunsets. But the sunset had only been a temporary distraction.

For most of the day, Nick had been trying to figure out what he could say if he sent Lorna an e-mail. It would have been easy to come up with an excuse for not meeting her if he'd written yesterday. He could have said he'd been called out to work or had car trouble or some family emergency—any number of things that would have prevented him arriving at the Galleria at the agreed-upon meeting time. Any of those excuses would have sounded reasonable. After all, he had no way to contact her except through e-mail so he couldn't possibly have let her know he couldn't make it.

But he hadn't written her yesterday, because when he'd come home after that fiasco at the Galleria, he had arrived at the reluctant conclusion that it would be best if he never contacted her again.

Hell, what was the point? He had to be realistic. Now that he knew Lorna was Sweet Stuff, it was clear there was no chance he could ever build a relationship with her in the real world. Any idiot could see that.

Nick DeSanto and Lorna Hathaway?

That was a joke.

For one thing, she didn't like him. She'd made that abundantly clear. But the overriding reason was they came from totally different worlds. Her wealth and position as an owner of the company he worked for was an insurmountable obstacle, even if he *could* win her over in person.

No. A relationship with Lorna was a pipe dream. It would never work. The best thing he could do now would be to disappear from her life.

That was his decision yesterday, and after he'd made it, he was filled with deep regret. He felt especially bad about the hurt she would probably feel, but he told himself she was better off by him making a clean break. She'd feel bad for a while and wonder what had happened, but she'd get over it. It wasn't like they'd had a big romantic thing going and he'd broken her heart. They were just Internet buddies.

Yet after a restless night followed by a miserable day where he kept seeing Lorna the way she'd looked at the Galleria—that hopeful light in her eyes as she scanned the crowd, the way she'd practically begged him to leave so she wouldn't jinx her meeting with Coach—Nick changed his mind. And his change of heart wasn't entirely due to his concern over Lorna's feelings. He finally had to admit to himself that he didn't want to give up his friendship with her. Even if that friendship had to remain anonymous forever, it still meant a lot to him, and he knew it meant something to her, too.

So he'd decided that today he somehow had to make amends. And the first step was to write her and give her a plausible reason for not showing up for their meeting. But even though he'd made that decision hours ago, he still hadn't come up with the right words to use.

Maybe he just needed to sit down and start writing. Maybe the right words would come. So as the last daylight faded from the sky, he went to his desk and opened his e-mail program. After a moment, he created a new message and began to write.

Dear Sweet Stuff,
You probably think I'm the world's biggest jerk for not showing up yesterday and not writing you to tell you why, but

Dammit!
Nick pressed the backspace key until everything but *Dear Sweet Stuff* was deleted. After a moment, he made another attempt.

The reason I didn't show up yesterday was because we had another emergency at work, and by the time I finally got out of there, it was so late, I was exhausted and thought I'd just wait and write today

Oh, hell.
She knew he had access to his e-mail account at work. She'd see right through that flimsy excuse and realize it was a lie. If he wanted to use that excuse, he'd have to say their computer system had gone down. He quickly discarded that idea. That was too many coincidences.

Once more he deleted what he'd written. After staring at the blank e-mail awhile, he began one more time.

I'm very sorry about yesterday, more sorry than you will ever know. I wish I could explain, but right now, I can't. Someday I hope I can tell you everything. I know it's asking a lot, to just take me on trust, but I'm asking it, anyway. Until I can fully explain, can you forgive me for not being there when I said I would be? Your friendship means a lot to me, so I hope you will.

Nick looked at the message a long time. Should he say something about meeting another time? That would be tricky, because he knew it wasn't going to be possible unless something changed drastically. No. He'd better not. Best to just leave the e-mail the way it was. Right now, it was the best he could do.

Signing the message simply, with just his online name—Coach—he pressed Send before he could change his mind.

When Lorna came home from church and there was still no message from Coach, she knew she would be unable to stand being home all day by herself. But what could she do to fill the day?

She didn't want to call Claudia because Claudia and John deserved to have time alone, and she'd been spending too much time with them lately. They were not responsible for keeping her entertained.

She thought longingly of Morgan Creek, and for

the first time in the weeks since she'd moved away, she wished she were there. The loneliness that had plagued her off and on for the past year gave her an empty sensation in her stomach. Even Buttercup, who was rubbing against her legs, didn't help to assuage her feelings, which suddenly seemed overwhelming.

It's your own fault if you're lonely. You were going to join a church group or sign up for some classes, and you've done neither.

Okay, so she'd rectify that omission as soon as possible. But that didn't solve the problem of how she was going to fill the day.

She didn't feel like going shopping or to a museum, but she had to do *something,* so she finally decided to go and see a movie. She'd never gone to a movie by herself before, but she knew lots of women did, especially during the day. It might feel awkward at first, walking into a theater alone, but so what? It would be dark. No one would know her. It wasn't a big deal.

Hurriedly changing into a pair of jeans and a T-shirt, she slung her handbag over her shoulder and headed off to the theater. The movie she'd chosen— a thriller with Ashley Judd—managed to take Lorna's mind off Coach and the whole letdown of yesterday for a couple of hours, but when it was over and she was on her way home, she began thinking about him and their nonmeeting again.

Why hadn't he come?

And why hadn't he written to her since then?

But just as there had been no answer to these questions the first hundred times she'd asked them, there were no answers now.

Although she told herself not to get her hopes up, the first thing she did when she walked into the house was head for her computer. Disappointment settled like a stone in her chest when the only new e-mail waiting for her was from her sister Chloe, who only wanted to discuss Thanksgiving. That was so typical of Chloe, Lorna thought. To want to finalize plans for a holiday that was still two months off. Lorna's life could be falling apart. Shoot, the whole *world* could be falling apart, but Chloe would still want to make sure she knew exactly who would be coming to her house for Thanksgiving dinner.

Completely dispirited, Lorna filled the remainder of the day with laundry and dinner—she even made a new chicken spaghetti recipe. Then she fixed herself a tall glass of iced tea and settled into her favorite chair with a new book by Elizabeth Berg, a favorite author. But she was too preoccupied to concentrate on the story and finally put the book down. She purposely did not check her e-mail again until she was ready for bed. No sense in adding salt to the wound.

She tried not to get her hopes up as she logged on to her Jamboree account.

Several messages downloaded.

Her heart leaped.

One of them was from Coach!

"Oh, ye of little faith," she chided herself aloud. "You should have known he had a perfectly good reason for not showing up yesterday. Now you'll find out what happened."

Smiling, she opened the e-mail and began to read.

I wish I could explain, but right now I can't. Someday I hope I can tell you everything.

Reading this, she frowned. Why didn't he just say what happened? What could be so bad that he couldn't tell her?

But then she read on.

I know it's asking a lot, to just take me on trust, but I'm asking it, anyway. Until I can fully explain, can you forgive me for not being there when I said I would be? Your friendship means a lot to me, so I hope you will.

Take him on trust.

Trust.

She sat back in her chair. *Trust.* Did she trust

Coach? Trust meant believing in someone's character. Believing they wouldn't lie to you. Believing that your confidence in them wasn't misplaced.

Trust.

She wanted to trust him.

Why hadn't he said something about arranging another meeting? Something was wrong, obviously. And yet, he'd said their friendship was important to him. That he was sorrier than she'd ever know.

Maybe she was a fool, but his words had the ring of truth. Taking a deep breath, she made up her mind.

Hitting Reply, she wrote:

Of course I forgive you. We're friends, aren't we? I'll admit I was disappointed when you didn't show up. In fact, I was afraid maybe you came and saw me talking to this guy from work and then left. I'm glad to know that didn't happen.

She stopped short at mentioning meeting again. Since he hadn't mentioned it, she wouldn't, either.

The next move was up to Coach.

Nick left for Morgan Creek at seven-thirty Monday morning. His appointment with Bryce wasn't until eleven, but he wanted to be sure he got to the plant in plenty of time. Now that he'd heard back from Lorna, and she was okay with his lack of explanation about Saturday, he was relaxed and enjoyed the ride into the Hill Country.

In a way, it was perfect timing for him to be going to the home office. Having a day before he had to see Lorna face-to-face couldn't hurt, for he still hadn't figured out exactly how he wanted to proceed with their in-person relationship. He'd stopped calling it their *real* relationship, even in his thoughts, because their online relationship was as real as any he'd ever had. In fact, it was more real, or at least, it had more depth.

It was odd, but there was something about e-mail and instant messaging that made you feel safe. You could say things to each other that you'd never say face-to-face. And not divulging their identities had only increased that sense of security so that they'd felt even freer to reveal their most intimate thoughts and fears.

He remembered how she'd once told him what a blow her divorce had been to her self-confidence. How she'd considered the breakup a personal failure. How she'd felt that everyone was talking about her and feeling sorry for her.

I have a great career, but that hasn't carried over to my personal life, she'd written. *I always think other people know some secret I don't know.*

Now that he matched what she'd said anonymously to the Lorna Hathaway he'd known for years, he realized that his perception of Lorna had been completely wrong. Things she'd said or not said that he'd taken as snobbery now translated to an inner uncertainty of her own self-worth.

If she knew who Coach really was, would she view *him* differently, too?

He was still thinking about Lorna when he arrived at the plant at 10:20 a.m. Before going over to Bryce's office, Nick decided to pop into the plant and say hello to Howard Welby, his counterpart in Morgan Creek.

"Hey, Nick! Long time no see." Howard's red face was wreathed in smiles as he shook Nick's hand. "How're things goin' in the big, bad city?"

"Except for cooler problems, pretty good," Nick said. He liked Howard, who was a big, affable man who got along with everyone. The two men were standing by the sponge mixer, and from the smell, Nick knew they were currently mixing the sponge for sourdough bread.

"You come to see Bryce?"

"Yeah."

"Let's walk outside where it's not so noisy," Howard said.

Nick removed his hairnet when they left the plant floor, but Howard—who would be returning soon—left his on. Howard patted his shirt pocket, then smiled sheepishly. "I quit smokin' six months ago, but I still forget sometimes."

Nick nodded sympathetically. "I know. I quit five years ago, and sometimes I still crave a cigarette."

"So you've got Lorna Hathaway in Houston now, huh?"

"Yeah. She came about a month ago."

"How's it workin' out?"

With anyone else, Nick would have suspected a hidden agenda in the question, but he knew Howard well enough to know the man didn't have a devious bone in his body. "It's working out well. She does her share."

"Yeah, she always pulled her weight here. For that matter, so does Bryce." Howard frowned. "Not like the old man, neither one of them."

Nick had only met Jonathan Hathaway once, but he'd heard enough about him to know what kind of person he was, and nothing he'd heard was good.

"They're not like their mother, either," Howard continued.

Nick had never met Kathleen Hathaway, and he was curious. "What's she like?"

"You never met her?"

"No."

"Hoity-toity, that's what my grandmother would have called her. Thinks she's better'n us common folks. Fact is, I can't remember when she last set foot in the plant. Must be at least ten years. She's been to the offices, but mix with the workers? Not on your life.

"Now, the old woman, the grandmother, she was comin' over here, checkin' on things, watchin' what we were doin', learnin' new techniques up until she went into her wheelchair."

The old woman. Stella Morgan Hathaway. Nick had seen photos of her. She'd been beautiful in her younger years and even now was said to be elegant and imposing. He remembered another "conversation" via e-mail with Lorna where they'd talked about the person in their families they were closest to, and Lorna had said that aside from her younger sister, she was closest to her grandmother.

She approves of me, she'd written, *Lord knows why. I'm not as strong or courageous or smart as she is, but she seems to think I am....*

Nick remembered how he'd asked about her mother.

We're not close at all. She doesn't *approve of me.*

When Nick had questioned her further, she'd said she really didn't want to talk about her mother. *Our relationship, or lack of one, makes me sad. It'll never change, so there's no use dwelling on it.*

The things she'd said then made more sense to him now. And they also made him understand her better.

"So you goin' to talk to Bryce about a new cooler?"

Nick smiled. "What are you, Howard? A mind reader?"

"Doesn't take a genius to figure it out."

"Yeah, I have to. We can't take many more breakdowns without losing accounts. And with competition like Willoughby…"

Howard frowned. "Yeah, they're starting to infiltrate all our markets. You gonna talk to Bryce about doing some more specialty breads? Their ciabatta and focaccia are flyin' off the shelves, accordin' to my wife. In fact, she bought some the other day. For research purposes, of course."

"Yeah, I'm going to talk to him about that, too. I think we have to add to our lineup if we hope to stay competitive."

"I agree. I already suggested it to him, but it'll help if you do, too."

By now it was time for Nick to walk over to the office, so he said goodbye to Howard, and headed for the main building.

Every time Nick came to Morgan Creek, he was impressed by the lack of pretension in either Bryce Hathaway or his office surroundings. The room was comfortable and even had a conversation area with deep chairs and a coffee table, but it was basically no frills. And the man himself, while obviously well-educated and intelligent, was also no frills. Today he was dressed similarly to Nick—in khaki pants and a knit shirt. He welcomed Nick with a friendly smile, then invited him to have a seat.

They shook hands. "Have a good trip over?" Bryce asked.

"I did," Nick said.

They made small talk for a while, then Bryce said, "I know you want to talk to me about your cooler problem."

Nick grimaced. "Unfortunately." He went on to enumerate the recent incidences where the cooler had broken down. He had brought along a report of the money lost and waited until Bryce had had a chance to look it over before making his recommendation that they purchase a new cooler rather than continue to repair the existing one.

"I agree," Bryce said when Nick had finished.

Nick tried not to look surprised, but he was. He'd expected Bryce to play devil's advocate. This was almost too easy. "Good. I'm glad. I thought I'd have to sell harder."

"So what else?" Bryce asked.

Nick mentioned his conversation with Howard and their mutual feeling that Hathaway needed to add a few more specialty breads to their current lineup. Bryce also agreed with that suggestion. After that, they had a long discussion about Houston's quarterly sales figures and how they could improve the bottom line.

"How's my sister doing?" Bryce asked when they'd exhausted that topic.

Nick smiled. "I think she's doing great. She's definitely an asset to the Houston organization. But maybe you should ask her."

Bryce chuckled. "She tells me to quit acting like an older brother when I question her."

"That's what my sister always said."

"You know, I owe you an apology."

Nick frowned. "What for?"

"I didn't realize it at the time, but I should have asked you if you minded having Lorna in Houston."

Nick wondered if Lorna had mentioned what he'd said that time he'd told her he resented not being asked. "I admit it bothered me that you didn't, even though it's worked out okay."

Bryce met his gaze steadily. "Thanks for being honest. I give you my word I won't do anything like that again." He looked at his watch. "It's almost twelve-thirty. Ready for lunch? Mark Baxter, our new sales manager, is going to go with us."

"Good. I was hoping to meet him."

"This afternoon I want you to sit in on the marketing meeting."

"Okay."

"Then tonight," Bryce said, "Amy and I would like to have you for dinner at our house. You're staying overnight, right?"

"Yeah. Your secretary made a reservation for me at that new motel out on the interstate."

"Good."

As the two men walked over to the sales offices to get Mark Baxter, Nick thought how lucky he was to work for a man like Bryce. He knew Bryce liked him. Yet Nick couldn't help but wonder if Bryce would feel the same way about him if he knew about his relationship with Lorna.

Hell, he might think Nick was trying to work his way up the corporate ladder the easy way, by romancing the boss's sister.

Lorna had just climbed into bed when the phone rang. Seeing her brother's number on the caller ID pad, she decided to answer.

"Hi, Lorna. I didn't wake you, did I?" It was Amy.

"No. I was just about to read myself to sleep. What's up?"

"Well, I just had to call. Guess who we had for dinner tonight?"

"I have no idea. Who?"

"Nick DeSanto."

"Really? What did you think of him?"

"Lorna, I have to be truthful with you. I really liked him."

Lorna guessed she wasn't surprised. Everyone seemed to like Nick. Everyone but her. But she had to admit that lately she hadn't disliked him as much as she used to.

"I can't imagine why you don't like him," Amy was now saying.

"We just got off on the wrong foot, I guess. Must be something about me."

"Well, in your shoes, I'd see if I couldn't do something to change that. He's a hunk, Lorna."

Lorna rolled her eyes. "Yes, I know he's sexy, but—"

"But what?"

"The thing is, even if I were interested in him, and I'm not, he'd never, not in a million years, be interested in me. Trust me, I'm so not his type."

"You think so, huh?"

"I know so."

"Well, he sure seemed interested enough in you tonight."

"What do you mean? Was he *talking* about me?"

"You could say that."

"What did he say?" *And why did she care?*

"For one thing, he told Bryce you were doing a great job and were an asset to the Houston organization."

"Maybe he was just trying to butter Bryce up."

"Oh, Lorna, for heaven's sake. I thought you were through putting yourself down."

Lorna grinned. "It's a hard habit to break." Besides, maybe Nick *had* been buttering up Bryce.

"Then during dinner, he mentioned how much he liked Mark Baxter, and I told him Mark and Leslie had bought the house you used to own. Mark must have told him it was a Victorian, because he said he owns a Victorian in Houston that *he's* fixed up."

Lorna would never have pegged someone like Nick being interested in old houses. If she'd thought about the subject at all, she would have imagined him in a starkly contemporary condo or high-rise apartment or loft.

Coach, on the other hand, loved old houses, because they'd had many a discussion about the renovations they'd each done to theirs.

"He was also interested in hearing about how you and I met and became friends," Amy went on. "In fact, I'd say he was *very* interested."

"The more you know about your enemy, the better prepared you are to deal with him," Lorna said, only half joking.

"Honestly, Lorna, you make me *crazy* sometimes! I'm a good judge of people, and I'm telling you. That man is interested in you. Big time."

After they hung up, Lorna sat there a long time, digesting what Amy had told her. What was Nick's game, she wondered? Because no matter what Amy had said, Lorna knew Nick DeSanto was no more interested in her the way Amy thought he was than he would have been in a ninety-year-old woman. All she had to do to know this was true was remember the busty redhead he'd brought to the Cajun restaurant that night.

"I'm not his type," she said aloud. "And I never will be." When Buttercup, who was waiting for Lorna to get into bed so she could curl up next to her, meowed, Lorna laughed. "End of story!" she said. "Now let's go to bed."

Chapter Seven

When Lorna arrived at the plant on Wednesday, the first thing she noticed was Nick's black Toyota truck in the employee parking lot. So he was back from Morgan Creek. She wondered if he considered the trip a success. She had purposely refrained from calling Bryce to ask him what had transpired between the two of them. She knew it was important to act as if she were just a regular employee in Houston, especially if she wanted to keep her working relationship with Nick a good one. And that meant getting her information through normal channels.

Entering the plant, she headed straight up to the administrative level. She had to pass Nick's office to get to her own, and she waved at Karen as she went by.

"Oh, Miss Hathaway!"

Lorna stopped. She had tried, without success, to get Karen to call her Lorna. "Yes?"

"Nick would like to see you."

"Oh, okay." Lorna walked into Karen's office. Nick's door was closed.

"Can I get you some coffee?" Karen asked.

"That would be great."

"Just go on in. He's expecting you."

Lorna knocked on Nick's door, then opened it. "You wanted to see me?"

He looked up from whatever it was he'd been reading and smiled. "Yes, I did. Have you got some time to talk?"

"Sure."

"Come in, then. Have a seat. Do you want some coffee?"

"Karen's getting me some." He sure was being friendly this morning.

A few seconds later, Karen appeared with a steaming mug of coffee. Once she was gone, with the door closed behind her, Nick spoke. "I wanted to tell you about my trip to Morgan Creek. But first I wanted to apologize for Saturday."

Lorna tried not to show her surprise. "You don't owe me an apology."

"Yes, I do. You were waiting for someone, and I horned in. Then when you asked me to leave, I didn't."

Lorna had had awhile to think about the run-in with Nick on Saturday. She smiled ruefully. "I overreacted. But I appreciate the apology."

"Then we're okay?"

Something about the way he was looking at her made her feel unsettled. "Of course, we're okay."

"Good." He smiled again. "I'd like for us to get along better, Lorna."

God, his eyes were gorgeous, she thought distractedly. She'd always wanted brown eyes, probably because everyone in her family had blue ones. "I—I'd like that, too."

Just then his intercom buzzed, saving her from having to say anything else. With an apologetic gesture, he picked up the phone, saying, "Yes, Karen?" After listening a moment, he said, "Lorna, I'm sorry, I've got a call from a client that I have to take. But I do have a lot I want to discuss with you. Can you come back about eleven?"

"Sure, no problem."

Lorna headed off to her office where she and Marilyn spent the morning reviewing forms and procedures for processing claims with their new health insurance carrier. Before she knew it, it was eleven and time to go back to Nick's office.

They spent the next hour discussing his trip to Morgan Creek. By twelve, Lorna's stomach was starting to rumble. She hadn't eaten much for breakfast, and she was hungry. As if he knew exactly what she was thinking, Nick said, "I don't know about you, but I'm starving. Want to go grab some lunch?"

He was just full of surprises today. "Sure."

He suggested Carlita's, a little Mexican restaurant nearby, one Lorna hadn't tried but had heard good things about. The parking lot was crowded when they arrived. It was obviously a popular place.

"Hey, Nick, good to see you again," the hostess, a pretty Hispanic woman, said as they walked in the door.

Nick gave her an appreciative smile. "You're looking good today, Sylvia."

Sylvia grinned. "Oh, you're such a flatterer!" But it was obvious she was pleased by the compliment.

In the past, Lorna would have mentally rolled her eyes at what she would have perceived as Nick's blatant flirting. Today, though, she saw his friendliness as something different: a genuine appreciation of women.

Had she misjudged him all this time?

Had it been her own insecurities when it came to men that had made her see him as something other than he really was?

The questions troubled Lorna. She had always considered herself a sensible woman with a good head on her shoulders, someone who made careful, considered decisions. But her gigantic mistake in marrying Keith had changed her and colored her perceptions, especially when it came to men. Maybe she *had* misjudged Nick.

"You're in luck. I have one booth left," Sylvia said, grabbing two menus and beckoning them to follow her.

Nick laughed. "Come on, admit it, you saved a booth for me."

Sylvia laughed and looked at Lorna. "Oh, he is so full of himself! Do not believe him. I had no idea he was coming today."

Lorna smiled. She liked Sylvia.

Lorna slid into the booth, and Nick sat opposite her. Soon they had a basket of warm chips and a bowl of salsa in front of them.

"I love this stuff," Nick said, dipping a chip into the salsa.

"Me, too," Lorna said. "Almost too much."

"Yeah, they're supposed to be bad for you, but what the hell. We can't be good all the time."

Lorna grinned. "So you're saying you're good most of the time?"

He laughed. "I try."

Their waiter, a young man who introduced himself as Joaquin, came to take their drink order.

"You're new, aren't you?" Nick said.

Joaquin nodded. "I was lucky. My cousin helped

me get this job." He looked at Lorna. "Lots of people want to work here. It's a good place."

Once he was gone, Nick said, "So what do you think of Houston now that you've been here awhile?"

Lorna smiled. "I like it."

"It's a big change from Morgan Creek."

"Yes, but most of the changes are good ones."

Nick ate another couple of chips. "You know, when I first found out you were coming to Houston, I thought you were coming to spy on me."

Lorna's mouth dropped open. "You didn't."

He grimaced. "I did."

"But Nick, that's…that's crazy. Bryce would never do anything like that. If he thought you weren't doing a good job, he'd come right out and tell you."

"I know that. It's just that…" He shrugged. "You have to admit that you gave up a great position to take something that's much lower in status, and I couldn't figure out why."

"Have you figured it out now?"

"I don't know. I guess it's possible you just wanted a change."

"That's exactly why I moved." Lorna hesitated, then decided to be completely honest with him. "The truth is, my personal life was the pits. And in Morgan Creek there wasn't much opportunity to change that. I knew I had to go somewhere where I could meet people. Have a chance to build the kind of life I want."

"And have you?"

"Have I what?"

"Met people?"

"I'm working on it. It's not as easy as I thought it would be."

"What about that guy I saw you with at Burney's?"

Lorna made a face. "He was a blind date."

"And?"

"And not my type."

"He seemed nice. And he seemed to really like *you.*"

"He was nice. Too young, though. It was all my sister's idea. I hate blind dates. They never turn out well." Later, she would never know what made her add, "But you wouldn't know about blind dates."

"What makes you say that?"

"A guy like you? Women fall all over you."

He gave her a strange look. "Where did you get *that* idea?"

"Oh, come on, Nick, I've got eyes."

"Well, you're wrong. Women do not fall all over me. And I've had a few blind dates in my life, so I know exactly what you're talking about."

Lorna wasn't sure she believed him, but she'd give him points for trying to downplay his sex appeal.

"So what about the guy you were waiting for on Saturday? He wasn't a blind date, was he?"

"I—" Lorna stopped because just then their waiter returned with their drinks and wanted to know if they were ready to order. Nick had already recommended the house specialty, seafood enchiladas, which they both ordered. When the waiter left, Nick said, "You never answered my question."

"About the friend I was meeting on Saturday, you mean?"

"Yes."

"No, he…he wasn't a blind date." And technically speaking, Coach *wouldn't* have been a blind date. After all, she knew Coach. She knew him as well as, or better than, some people she'd known all her life.

"So he *did* show up on Saturday?"

Lorna had just taken a drink of her iced tea, so she had a moment before she had to answer. "No, he didn't make it. He…was unavoidably detained."

Nick frowned. "I hope he made it up to you."

"He apologized. He couldn't help missing our date." Then, because he was still frowning, she said, "Don't tell me you've never had to cancel a date."

"Sure, I've had to cancel dates, but I always cancel *before* the appointed time. I'd never let someone wait and wait and just not show up. Why didn't he call you?"

Lorna knew she could say this was none of his business, but he seemed sincerely concerned for her feelings. "The truth is, he couldn't call me. He…he doesn't know my name."

"Doesn't know your *name?*"

Lorna shook her head. "He's never really met me. Not in person, anyway."

Nick stared at her. "But you said he wasn't a blind date."

"He wouldn't have been. The thing is, we've been friends for months, even though we've never met in person. I—I met him on the Internet."

"On the Internet?"

"Don't look so surprised. People *do* meet on the Internet, you know."

"Yes, I know, but not women like you."

"What do you mean, not women like me?"

"Lorna, come on. You're a beautiful woman. You're smart, you're rich. Why would you have to meet men on the Internet?"

"It's not like that."

"It's not?"

"Don't look so skeptical. It's *not*. We…we met playing this game that's like Scrabble. And we got to be friends."

"But he doesn't know your name."

"No. We decided not to identify ourselves. I—I thought it was more prudent."

"At least you were sensible about *that.* "

They stopped talking as their food arrived and didn't resume the conversation until their waiter had refilled their water glasses, asked if they wanted anything else, then left them alone again.

Nick waited until Lorna had a chance to sample her enchiladas, which were, as Nick had said they would be, exceptionally good. Then he said, "So what made you decide to meet this Internet friend of yours?"

"I don't know. He's…he's so nice. I like him very much. And he suggested meeting." She met Nick's eyes. "Do you think I'm crazy?"

He shook his head. "No, but I'm glad you picked a public place."

"That's what Claudia said. In fact, she and John—that's her husband—said to call them immediately if I felt the least bit nervous."

"That's good. I'm glad someone was looking out for you. Hell, Lorna, the guy could've turned out to be a real weirdo."

"I know, but I don't think he is."

"People can misrepresent themselves on the Internet. They do it every day."

"I know, but—"

"But you're going to meet him another time, aren't you?"

Lorna shrugged. "Maybe." She ate some of her enchiladas. "If he wants to."

"If *he* wants to? You mean he didn't suggest meeting again?"

She shook her head.

"If he had any brains at all, he would," he said softly.

Lorna didn't know what to say. Her heart fluttered in her chest as her gaze locked with his. What was going on here? Was Nick *flirting* with her?

"What will you do if he does suggest meeting again?" he said after a moment.

"I don't know," she admitted truthfully. "I'll probably go." Her heart was still going too fast.

He nodded. After that, they both ate quietly for a while. Lorna's heart finally settled down, and she decided she'd been flattering herself to think Nick was flirting with her. Why would he flirt with *her?* It was just his nature to compliment women. Hadn't she decided that already? That he just liked *all* women?

"So," he finally said in a teasing voice, "what other things have you been doing for fun? Besides blind dates and meeting guys on the Internet?"

Grateful that he'd lightened the atmosphere, Lorna said, "I've started jogging in Memorial Park."

"I said, for fun."

Lorna grinned. "Running *is* fun."

"Actually, I've been thinking about running there myself. When do you go?"

"After work usually, although on the weekends, I go early. Before it gets too hot."

He nodded thoughtfully. "Maybe I'll see you there sometime. Although probably not on Saturdays. That's the only day I have to work on my house."

"That's something you and my Internet friend have in common. He likes old houses, too."

Nick gave her a funny look. "How'd you know I like old houses?"

Too late, Lorna realized her mistake. She could feel her face heating. Damn, she hated the way she blushed when she was embarrassed. "I, um, actually, my sister-in-law, Amy, mentioned it when we talked last night."

"You were talking about me, huh?" His eyes twinkled.

"Well, yes, she mentioned that you'd been there for dinner."

"It was a nice evening. I liked her very much."

Lorna smiled. "Everyone likes Amy. She liked you, too."

"Your brother's a lucky man."

"Yes, he is. When his first wife died, we weren't sure he'd ever be happy again, but then Amy came along. It's worked out so well."

"That baby of theirs is beautiful. So are the other girls."

Lorna's smile turned bittersweet. "Yes, they're darlings, all of them." Her eyes met his again. "I miss them. That's part of the downside of moving away. I used to see them practically every day. Now it'll be weeks, maybe even months, between visits."

"They won't forget you."

"No, but it'll never be the same."

By now Lorna had finished her lunch, too. Nick signaled for the waiter to bring their check.

"Do *you* have any nieces or nephews?" Lorna asked.

Nick smiled. "Yep. My sister has two boys and my older brother and his wife have two girls. And my younger brother's wife is expecting."

"My sister's expecting, too!"

"Your younger sister? The one who lives here?"

"Yes. She's so excited. It's their first."

"She got married recently, didn't she?"

"Yes, in February. They eloped."

"Really?"

Lorna grinned. "You can't imagine the ruckus *that* caused. I thought my mother would have a stroke, and my *grandmother!* She was furious with them. Hathaway women do not elope, you know. It just isn't *done*." She started to laugh. "Oh, it was priceless. I was never so proud of Claudia."

"I think you have a bit of a rebel in you."

"Maybe I do. It's been tamped down for quite a while now, but who knows? Maybe it's coming back."

By now the waiter had brought the check and while Nick took care of the bill, Lorna excused herself to go to the ladies' room. When she returned, Nick was waiting by the door. "Ready?"

They didn't talk on the short drive back to the plant. When they got there, Nick said, "Thanks for joining me today. I enjoyed it."

"Me, too." And Lorna meant it.

Saying goodbye, Nick left her to go talk to Cal

Lopez. As Lorna climbed the steps to the office level, she thought about how quickly things could change. Yesterday if she'd been asked, she would have said she no longer disliked Nick DeSanto, but she couldn't imagine herself ever being friends with him. Today she felt just the opposite.

And yet…there was still a small part of her that didn't entirely trust him. This change of heart he seemed to have had toward her…could it have been brought about because he'd realized, after the trip to Morgan Creek, that it was to his benefit to win her over?

Did he want something from her?

All those compliments today. He *had* to want something. Why hadn't she realized that sooner? Before she'd exposed herself so thoroughly?

She especially wished she hadn't told him about Coach. Well, it was too late now. She'd told him, and she couldn't take the words back. But one thing she *could* do. She could be a lot more cautious around Nick in the future.

That night, when Lorna walked into her house— dripping wet from a forty-five minute run—her phone was ringing. She debated just ignoring it until she'd had a chance to shower and change, then thought she'd at least check the Caller ID.

It was her sister Chloe.

Lorna sighed, but she answered. "Hold on a minute, Chloe. Let me get a towel to dry off. I just got in from jogging."

"Jogging *outside?* Why don't you buy yourself a treadmill?"

Lorna made a face, glad Chloe couldn't see her. "I'm going to put the phone down for a minute. I'll be right back." She didn't wait to see if Chloe agreed or not. Instead, she set down the phone and headed for the bathroom. Once she'd dried herself off, she hung the towel around her neck, picked up the phone and walked toward the kitchen with the intention of retrieving a bottle of water from the refrigerator. "Okay," she said to her sister. "I'm dry now."

"Has Mother called you?" Chloe said.

"Mother? No. I haven't talked to her in a week. Why? Is something wrong?" Surely Amy or Bryce would have called her if something *was* wrong.

"You could say that."

"What?" Lorna said, alarmed now.

"Mother is getting married again."

"What?" Lorna stopped in the act of twisting the top off her bottle of water. "To *whom?* I didn't even know she was dating anyone."

"She wasn't. This whole thing is crazy, Lorna. Just crazy. Get this. She's going to marry her *masseur!*"

"Her *masseur!*"

"Yes. Some young stud that she's been going to

for a whole two months. It's disgusting. He's *my* age. Thirty-eight! And she's sixty-five. I know she doesn't look it, thanks to all her cosmetic surgery, but the fact remains that she is. God, Lorna, everyone is going to laugh their fool heads off over this. It's a cliché. Rich, silly, older woman loses her head over handsome young stud. How stupid is that? Couldn't she just have *sex* with him? Does she have to *marry* him?"

Now that Lorna had had a chance to digest Chloe's startling revelation, she was starting to feel amused. Proper Kathleen Bryce Hathaway was thumbing her nose at the world? The same Kathleen Bryce Hathaway who, for years, had been so obsessed about her social position? The very same Kathleen Bryce Hathaway that had practically written the book on proper behavior? Lorna bit back a smile. "What does Grandmother have to say about all this?"

"What do you think? She's *furious*. She told Mother to get out of the house if she was going to behave in such a scandalous way."

"Oh, my." For one of the few times in her adult life, Lorna felt sympathetic toward her mother.

"Lorna, this is a *disaster*. We're going to be a laughingstock."

"Oh, come on, Chloe, it's not *that* big a deal, is it? I mean, older women have been making fools of themselves over younger men for longer than we've been alive, and the world hasn't come to an end."

"Easy for *you* to say. You don't live here. And you don't have a husband or children to worry about."

"I don't know what one has to do with the other." Lorna tried not to feel hurt by Chloe's insensitive comment, but she did.

"We have a certain position to uphold in the community, Lorna. Surely you realize that."

"Now you sound exactly like Mother."

"Yes! That's the point! What is she *thinking?* Maybe he's drugged her or something. This is just not like her."

"For heaven's sake. Listen to yourself. I'm sure she's not drugged." Drugged on sex, maybe, Lorna thought, laughing in spite of herself.

"I don't know why you find this so amusing."

"I'm sorry, Chloe. But you know, it's not cancer. It's not the death of a child. And it's not war. It's just *sex.* Normal sex. Something Mother hasn't had in a long time, I'll bet." In fact, Lorna was sure of it. Her father had been an alcoholic for a long time before his death, and alcoholics cared about one thing only: booze. Not to mention the fact that alcohol rendered many of them impotent. Realizing abruptly that she'd carried this thought as far as she'd cared to, she said, "Don't you think she deserves to be happy? No matter where that happiness comes from?"

"Oh, you're just as bad as Claudia."

"You've already called Claudia?"

"I tried calling you, but you'd already left work, and then you didn't answer your cell phone. I had to talk to someone."

Lorna always locked her cell phone in her car when she jogged. "So when is this happy event taking place?"

"Mother said they're going to Vegas. Tomorrow. Then they're going to Europe. They'll be gone a couple of months, she said. Maybe longer. I don't know, and right now, I don't care. I'm just thankful she doesn't control the company *or* our portion of it. At least Dad did something right."

Yes, Lorna was glad the company was protected, too. Although, unlike Chloe, she thought her mother had a perfect right to do whatever she wanted to do in her personal life, she didn't want to see her squander the family fortunes while she was doing it. "So where is Mother now?"

"Apparently she's taken a suite at The Lake House." The Lake House was a privately owned resort hotel on a small lake about ten miles northwest of Morgan Creek. "And *he's* moved in with her."

"What's this man's name?"

"Julian. His last name is something like Thanos. He's Greek. She said he plans to take her to Greece." Chloe made a disparaging sound. "That's a joke. We all know who's going to be paying for everything."

After they'd hung up, Lorna thought about calling

Bryce, and then Claudia, but she wanted a shower more than she wanted to hear their version of the story.

The calls could wait, she decided.

Nothing was likely to change in the next hour, and after a shower and something to eat, she'd be better prepared for the conversations to come.

Wasn't life interesting? she thought as she stripped and entered the shower stall. You thought you knew someone, and then they did something so totally out of character that you realized you didn't know them, after all.

We all have secrets and hidden desires.

Even me.

Chapter Eight

TO: Coach1012@bayoucity.net
FROM: SweetStuff@jamboree.net
SUBJECT: Life's Surprises
Hi, Coach! I have so many things to tell you, I hardly know where to start. My big news is, my mother is getting married again! I can hardly believe it. My older sister called tonight to tell me. Turns out my mother has fallen for her masseur, who is nearly thirty years younger than she is. My sister (and my grandmother) is freaked out over it, but I kind of think it's funny. Oh, I'd hate to see my mother get taken in by someone only interested

in her money (she has quite a bit), but I don't think that's going to happen. My mother is pretty smart. If she spends money on this guy, it'll be because she thinks it's worth it, not because she's blinded by his charms. Personally, I think if being with him makes her happy, she should go for it. She sure wasn't happy with my father. I know we've talked about this before, because you said you understood, that you had an aunt married to an alcoholic, and she was miserable for years before she finally got the courage to leave him. It's too bad, though, that she couldn't have waited longer. My father has barely been dead a year. On the other hand, what difference does it really make? This new marriage would have caused a scandal no matter when it took place.

After I talked to my sister, I called my brother and my other sister. Then I finally called my mother—who's moved out of the family home, BTW—and had one of the most satisfying conversations with her that I've ever had in my entire life. She sounded so happy, Coach. It just made me feel good to listen to her. She said she knew most people would think she was crazy, would maybe even laugh at her, but she didn't care. She said her fiancé is wonderful and that he makes her feel good. She said she'd never been so happy in her life. The truth is, by the time we finished our conversation, I was jealous.

They're getting married this weekend in Las Vegas. When I told her I'd like to be there, she said she was touched, but she was also firm, saying she thought it would be better to just do it without any fanfare. After the ceremony, they are going to Europe for several months. He is from Greece, and he wants her to see his country and meet his family.

My second piece of news concerns that guy at work, the one I told you about? Something has happened. I don't know what, but he is acting very different toward me lately. Today he even took me to lunch, and I had the nicest time. I've been thinking that maybe I've misjudged him. He's actually a pretty decent guy.

Oh, and you two have something in common, it turns out. He, too, likes old houses. He bought a Victorian in the Heights and he's fixed it up. Where is your house located? Is it a Victorian, too? Who knows? You could be a neighbor of his.

BTW, I've been wondering about Maggie and how she's doing. You'd mentioned that she was limping last week. Did you take her to the vet? What did the vet say?

Well, it's awfully late, and I'm tired. Sorry I didn't get online tonight to play WordMaker. Did you play? See you online tomorrow, I hope.

Your buddy,

Sweet Stuff

TO: SweetStuff@jamboree.net
FROM: Coach1012@bayoucity.net
SUBJECT: Re: Life's Surprises
Dear Sweet Stuff,

From everything you've told me about your mother, to say I was surprised at your news is an understatement. I know you said your mother seems to be well aware of the pitfalls of this relationship, but I can't help hoping she really *is* being cautious.

Did you happen to talk to her about a prenup? If she has quite a bit of money, a prenup would only be sensible. And if this guy is on the up-and-up and isn't marrying her for her money, he should have no hesitation over signing one. Other than that, I say, whatever floats her boat. Everyone deserves to have some happiness in life, and if this man makes her happy, what's the harm?

As to your second piece of news, so your co-worker has decided to be nice to you, huh? What brought that on? And are you sure you can trust him? Although, if he likes old houses, he must have redeeming qualities.

Maggie's doing fine. Thanks for asking. I did take her to the vet. He couldn't see any reason for the limp, which has since disappeared. Tonight when I got home she was leaping around just like she used to do when she was a pup. She's always so glad to see me, especially when I have to work late. Sometimes I feel bad about her being alone so much, but she doesn't seem to mind. She's got a nice fenced yard with plenty of room to run and a screened-in back porch with a dog door so she can get in out of the rain or whatever anytime she wants to. Actually, she's got a pretty darned cushy life.

No, I didn't play WordMaker tonight. I logged on, but I saw you weren't there, and I had a lot of paperwork to take care of, so I logged right off again. Not sure about tomorrow night. I've been invited to my sister's house to celebrate her oldest boy's tenth birthday, so it may be too late to play after I get home. But I'll try to get online Friday. If not, I'll be there for sure on the weekend.
Take care,
Coach

TO: Coach1012@bayoucity.net
FROM: SweetStuff@jamboree.net
SUBJECT: Re: Re: Life's Surprises
Hi, Coach,
Thanks for the suggestion about the prenup. I called my mother again tonight and suggested she consider having one, and she said she'd already taken care of it, that he had even agreed with her. So that's a relief, knowing she'll be protected. Now I can wholeheartedly be happy for

her and hope she has a wonderful life with her new husband.

Oh, and I'm so glad Maggie's fine. I know how worried I am when Buttercup is under the weather. Thing is, our pets become just like our children, don't they? They're so dependent on us and give us such unconditional love, they deserve only our best in return.

It's funny you should say what you did about that guy I work with. BTW, his name is Nick. It's easier to just call him by name than keep referring to him as "that guy from work," don't you think? <g> Well, Nick said pretty much the same thing about you as you did about him. He said I shouldn't be so trusting, that I don't really know you. But then he said if you like old houses you can't be all bad! LOL

Hope you're having fun at your nephew's birthday party tonight. That's the only thing I miss about living in Houston—being too far from my nieces to take part in all the activities and events concerning them.

Okay, I'll plan to log on to Jamboree Friday night around eight. If you can't make it, don't worry. I realize sometimes things come up that are unavoidable.

See you soon!

Sweet Stuff

* * *

"Happy Birthday, Kenny." Nick handed his nephew an envelope that contained a gift card for an electronics superstore as well as a crisp, new twenty-dollar bill. He knew Kenny would be in hog heaven picking out some new video games or DVDs.

"Gee, thanks, Uncle Nick." Kenny's dark eyes, the exact shade of Nick's, sparkled with excitement. He tore the envelope open, whooped when he saw the gift card and the money, then exuberantly threw his arms around Nick's waist. Nick hugged him back, thinking what a nice kid he was.

"Kenny, what did I tell you about waiting until we could all see your presents before you opened them?" Marie made a face at Nick, as if to say *what can you do?*

Nick grinned. Kenny and his brother Mark were as different as night and day. Whereas Kenny seemed to have jumping beans embedded in his body, Mark was quiet and calm, the kind of kid who actually thought before he acted. Marie and her husband Rich constantly teased that maybe they'd been given the wrong kid at the hospital. Of course, they could tease all they wanted, but Mark was the spitting image of his father, so it was clear he belonged, no matter how different he was from the boisterous Fabrizio and DeSanto families. Kenny, on the other hand, could've been Nick's kid; that's how much he resembled his uncle.

"So where you been lately?" Marie asked Nick once the gifts had been opened and the family had stuffed themselves on pizza, Kenny's favorite. "We missed you on Sunday."

"I told you, Marie," Nick's mother piped in. "Nicky had to go to the main plant in Morgan Creek early Monday morning."

Nick bit back a smile. His mother was like a bear where her children were concerned. She tolerated no criticism, protected her cubs fiercely, no matter what. Even when the imagined criticism took the form of an innocent question from another of her children, she still leaped to defend. "I spent Sunday afternoon getting all my ducks in a row," he explained to Marie, "so I'd be prepared for the meeting with my boss."

"How'd it go?" This came from Nick's brother Mike.

"Really good."

"So you're not worried about work anymore?" Mike said.

Nick frowned. "Who said I was worried?"

"You did. Doncha remember? Coupla weeks back when we were all at Ma's, you couldn't stop thinking about it."

Nick nodded. Mike was talking about right before Lorna came to work at the Houston plant. "I wasn't really worried then. There was just a lot going on.

Things have settled down since, even though we're still as busy. In fact, we're busier than ever. That's one of the things I talked to Bryce about, expanding the plant."

"Really?" Nick's father said. "Does that mean you'll be doing some hiring?"

"I'm sure we will."

"If you do, let me know, okay? Jimmy Donnelly's son has been looking for a better job for two months now with no luck."

Nick said he would. From there, the talk moved on to Mike's job, then Jay's, then the state of jobs in the country, and pretty soon the conversation became heated as it turned to politics. This was his cue to go, Nick decided. He'd been drawn into political discussions with his family once too often. The problem was, Nick's father and Nick's brothers were on opposite sides of the fence, and neither camp would ever give ground because each was convinced he was right. Good thing they all loved each other, Nick thought, because otherwise they might come to physical blows.

"I've got an early day tomorrow," he said, rising. "I'm gonna take off." He kissed his mother and sister, gave his father a hug and shook the hands of his brothers and brother-in-law. Before leaving, he went upstairs to the game room and said goodbye to all the kids, then he finally took off.

Driving home, he kept thinking about his family and then he started wondering what Lorna would think of them if she ever met them. Before discovering she was Sweet Stuff, he would have said she had nothing at all in common with them and would be like a fish out of water in their company.

Now, though, he wasn't so sure she *would* feel out of place. He remembered how many times she'd expressed envy over how close his family was and how well he got along with them. And they would probably like her, too, once they got over the difference in their backgrounds.

At that thought, he was brought up short. What in the hell was he thinking? Hadn't he already decided that he and Lorna could never be more than friends?

Get real, DeSanto. She's so far above you on the social and money scale, she might as well be on the moon.

His good mood evaporated.

He should have followed his first instinct after finding out Sweet Stuff's true identity. Instead, he was setting himself up for a fall. A big one.

On Friday, Lorna woke up with a sore throat and the certain knowledge she was coming down with a cold. She debated whether or not to go to work. She knew she shouldn't. Right now she was probably contagious and by going into the office, she'd just expose everyone else to whatever bug she had.

Besides, there wasn't anything pressing that required her presence at the office. She'd been planning to work on next year's budget, but that could easily wait a few days. Mind made up, she reset the alarm for eight, then closed her eyes and went back to sleep.

At eight she phoned Marilyn and told her why she wouldn't be in. "Oh, I hope you feel better soon," Marilyn said.

"You and me both," Lorna said.

"Don't worry about anything. Just get well."

"Thanks, but please do call if you need me."

After hanging up, Lorna put on water to boil for tea, dosed herself with Advil and made sure she had a new box of tissues for her bedside table. Briefly, she thought about making herself some toast, but right then she didn't much feel like eating. Maybe later, she thought. When her tea was ready, she added lemon and honey, then carried everything back to her bedroom.

By noon her head was pounding and felt like someone had stuffed it with cotton. She felt so lousy she could hardly drag herself out of bed to take more Advil.

Maybe she should call a doctor. But who? She didn't have a doctor in Houston. She thought about calling Claudia to ask about one, but she was afraid Claudia would insist on coming over, and that wasn't a good idea. Lorna sure didn't want to expose Claudia to whatever it was she had—certainly not in her pregnant state. Finally Lorna decided that if she didn't feel better tomorrow, she would ask Nick's secretary Karen to recommend a doctor. That settled, Lorna climbed back into bed.

After dozing on and off for most of the afternoon, she was just thinking about fixing herself something to eat when the doorbell rang.

Lorna sat up. Who on earth? If it was someone selling something, she wasn't going to open the door. Wrapping herself in her robe, she headed out to the foyer and looked through the peephole in the front door.

Her mouth dropped open. Nick! What in the world was *he* doing here?

The doorbell rang again.

Smoothing back her hair—which she was certain looked like a rat's nest from being in bed all day— Lorna undid the chain, then the dead bolt. Telling herself it didn't matter that she looked like death warmed over, she opened the door.

Nick smiled. "Hi."

"Hi."

"Karen told me you were sick, so I brought you some flowers…" He held out a bouquet of absolutely gorgeous pale pink roses.

Dumbfounded, Lorna gaped at the flowers. Pink roses had always been her favorite.

"They'll need to be put in water," he said with a chuckle.

"I—I, thank you," she managed, taking the bouquet from him. How had he known she loved pink roses?

"I also brought you some chicken soup." He held up a plastic container.

Lorna couldn't think what to say. That he was here was surprise enough. But that he'd brought her flowers and soup had rendered her practically speechless.

"May I come in?" he said.

"I— Oh, of—of course." Lorna backed up. Tried to get her thoughts under some semblance of control. He *couldn't* have known about the roses. His choice had to have been a lucky guess.

"I know I should have called first, but—"

"How did you know where I live?" she interrupted. Immediately, she realized that was a silly question. Of course, he knew where she lived. He had access to all the personnel records. All it would have taken was a couple of key strokes to give him the information.

"You should be in bed," he said. "You look awful."

"Thanks."

He grinned. "I didn't mean it that way. I meant you look as if you *feel* terrible."

"I do."

"C'mon, then, let's get you back to bed. Here, give me those flowers. I'll put them in water for you."

"I can do it." She walked back to the kitchen, and

he followed. "There's a crystal vase up there." She pointed to the top of the cupboard.

"I'll get it."

"I love pink roses. They're my favorite flower." She buried her face in the fragrant blossoms.

He smiled. "I'm glad you like them."

"They're beautiful," she said softly. She filled the vase with water and put the roses in.

"Now how about the soup? Want me to warm it up for you? My mother always says chicken soup is the only thing that'll help cure a cold."

Lorna felt a sneeze coming on and just managed to grab a tissue before it erupted. She blew her nose afterward, thinking how awful she must look with her red eyes and nose. "You don't have to do this, Nick. I can manage. Unless you needed to talk to me about something?"

"What have you had to eat today?" he said, ignoring her question.

Lorna grimaced. "Nothing. I really didn't feel up to it." She blew her nose again.

"Another thing my mother always says is 'feed a cold, starve a fever'." He frowned. "Or is it the other way around?"

Lorna couldn't help laughing. "I think 'feed a cold' is right."

"Then how about sitting down and letting me feed you?"

Too miserable to protest, she took the box of tissues from the counter and put them on the kitchen table. Then she sank down onto one of the chairs.

"Where are your bowls?" he asked.

Directing him to the right cupboard, Lorna sat and watched as he spooned soup into a bowl, then put the bowl into the microwave. While it heated, he leaned against the counter and looked at her.

"This is very nice of you," she said, reaching for another tissue.

"What are friends for?"

She blew her nose. "*Are* we friends?"

"I hope so."

Something about the way he was looking at her made Lorna uncomfortable. "What?" she finally said. "I know I look horrible."

"I don't think you look horrible at all. I think you look cute."

"Cute!" She started to laugh, but then sneezed.

While she was groping for another tissue, the microwave dinged, and Nick opened it. He took the dish towel hanging off the oven door, wadded it up and used it as a hot pad to remove the steaming bowl of soup. After placing it on the table in front of her, he began opening drawers. When he'd located her silverware, he pulled out a soup spoon and handed it to her. "Want some crackers or toast to go with that?" He seemed perfectly at home in her kitchen.

"I have some oyster crackers." She pointed to the pantry door. "They're in there."

Once everything was ready, he sat and watched her as she ate. Surprisingly, Lorna didn't feel awkward. In fact, it was kind of nice having him across the table. He didn't try to talk to her, just sat quietly until she'd finished all the soup. Then, motioning her to stay put, he cleaned up the table and washed out her bowl and spoon. "I'll just put the rest of this soup in the refrigerator, okay?" he said when he'd finished. The container was still about half-full.

"Okay, thanks. By the way, the soup was very good."

"I'm glad you liked it. I bought it from this little neighborhood deli near my house. Everything they sell is homemade." He smiled down at her. "Is there anything else I can do for you before I leave?"

She shook her head. "Not that I can think of."

"Well, you need to get back to bed, so I'm going to take off."

"All right." She stood, intending to walk him to the door.

"I can see myself out."

"I know, but I want to lock the door behind you."

Once there, he turned to face her. "You take care of yourself, Lorna."

"I will."

"And don't come back to work until you're completely well."

"I won't."

And then, astounding her because it was so unexpected, he leaned forward and kissed her cheek.

For a long time after he left, she kept touching her cheek and looking at the roses he'd brought her—which now occupied the place of honor on her dresser where she could see them from the bed—and wondering what in the world was going on. She wished she could trust this change in Nick's attitude toward her. She wanted to, yet there was a still a part of her that didn't believe his motive was friendship.

Nick wanted something from her.

The question was, could she keep her heart safe until she found out what that something was?

Chapter Nine

TO: SweetStuff@jamboree.net
FROM: Coach1012@bayoucity.net
SUBJECT: What's Up?
Dear Sweet Stuff,
What's going on? Haven't heard from you in days.
Hope nothing has happened.

TO: Coach1012@bayoucity.net
FROM: SweetStuff@jamboree.net
SUBJECT: Re: What's Up?
Hi, Coach,
I knew you were probably wondering what hap-

pened to me. I've been sick and just too miserable to even turn on my computer. I started feeling bad Thursday night, and by Friday morning it was ugly! <g> Since then I've been doctoring myself with Advil and chicken soup and hot tea. You're never going to believe this! The chicken soup came from Nick, that guy at work. I could hardly believe it myself. He just showed up here Friday afternoon. I wish I could believe he was on the up-and-up, but no matter how nice he is to me or how thoughtful, I can't banish the feeling that something is going on that I don't know about. Anyway, I will continue to be on guard, and one of these days, maybe I'll figure it out....

Lorna considered telling Coach about the roses, then changed her mind. She couldn't have said why; she just knew it probably wasn't a good idea.

Anyway, I'm feeling better tonight so I hope to go to work tomorrow. Don't know if I'll be online tomorrow night, though. I have a hunch by the time I put in eight hours at work, I'll be exhausted and ready to crash when I get home.

After Lorna sent the e-mail, she wondered if she should have mentioned Nick at all. Maybe Coach was tired of hearing about him. Maybe he'd think she was trying to make him jealous? Or worse—trying to force a meeting.

Was she?

Darn Nick, anyway. Before he started being nice to her, she never questioned anything she told Coach and she certainly never questioned her motives. Now everything had changed, and it was all Nick's fault.

And yet, was it fair to blame him? Didn't Coach have to bear some of the responsibility for the change in their relationship? If he'd shown up for their meeting that Saturday afternoon at the Galleria, everything would be different now.

As it was, they seemed to be in limbo, and darned if Lorna knew why. She'd expected him to suggest another meeting right away. But he hadn't.

Why?

Would he ever suggest meeting again?

More to the point, did she want him to?

Monday morning Lorna felt good enough to go to work. She still had the remnants of her cold, but she knew she was no longer contagious. By Wednesday, she felt she was operating at ninety percent capacity. And by Friday, she was once again her old self.

So Friday night, Lorna changed into her running clothes before leaving the office, then drove straight to Memorial Park. She parked on West Memorial Loop Drive, locked her car, and began to run along the jogging path. Although it was after six, it was still almost as hot as it had been midafternoon, so she didn't push too hard.

Twenty minutes into her run, she reached her personal halfway point and swung around to go back. By now she was dripping wet and, if not for the sweatband around her forehead, would have been blinded by perspiration running into her eyes. She was thinking longingly of a cool shower and some soothing foot lotion for her burning feet when a familiar voice called, "Lorna?"

Her head jerked up, and she blinked in surprise. Nick stood off to the side of the path.

Lorna wondered if her rapid heartbeat was all due to her run or if it had anything to do with how sexy Nick looked in his shorts that exposed muscular, tanned legs and his T-shirt that clung to an equally muscled chest. He was breathing as hard as she was.

"Hi," she said when she'd caught her breath. "Where'd you come from?"

"That way." He pointed to the western end of the park where she'd begun. "But I was getting ready to turn around. Mind if I run with you?"

"No, but you might want to go faster than me."

"I doubt that." He glanced down at her long legs. "You could probably leave me in the dust." Then he grinned. "Nice legs, Hathaway."

She smiled. "Yours aren't bad, either, DeSanto."

"Of course, your *hair* could use some work," he teased.

"Look who's talking." His hair was just as wet and plastered down as hers.

They settled into a comfortable pace—one where they were still getting a good workout but could carry on a conversation, too.

"So you meant it when you said you were going to start running?" she asked.

"Yeah. This is my third time this week."

She grimaced. "I haven't been for more than a week."

"Yeah, but you were sick."

"That's true."

"I figured I'd probably see you here today."

"You did?"

"Yeah, I just happened to be looking out my office window when I saw you getting into your truck. I noticed the change in clothes."

Lorna wondered if he'd planned to come out to the park before seeing her. He must have, otherwise he wouldn't have had his running clothes with him. And why would she think seeing her had anything to do with why he was here, anyway?

"Did you run when you lived in Morgan Creek?" he asked.

"Yes. But it was more difficult there. I had to run on back roads."

"That's dangerous. If there wasn't a trail here, I'd probably just stick with the gym."

"I hate gyms. All that testosterone makes me uncomfortable."

He laughed. "I know what you mean. Some of those guys are so damned *serious.* I just want to tell them to lighten up."

She grinned.

For a while after that, they ran companionably silent. Before long, they reached the place where Lorna had parked her SUV.

"Here's where I leave you. There's my truck," she said, coming to a stop.

"I'm finished, too." He wiped his face with the towel he had clipped to his waist. "It was fun running with you, Miss Hathaway. Nicer than running by myself."

Adopting his light tone, she said, "Thank you, Mr. DeSanto. I enjoyed it, too."

He smiled at her. "If I didn't need a shower so bad, I'd invite you out for a hamburger or something."

Lorna was surprised by the regret she felt. "Darn. Guess that means I'll have to go home and eat a Lean Cuisine again."

"Or," he said, "we could both go home, get cleaned up, and meet at Chuck's Ice House. Do you know Chuck's?"

"You mean that place right off Kirby near Richmond?"

"That's the one. Their burgers are fantastic. What do you say? We could meet at—" He looked at his watch. "Eight? Would that give you enough time?"

Lorna thought about how she was supposed to meet Coach online at eight. She'd been looking forward to that. And yet, she wanted to go to Chuck's with Nick. In fact, it surprised her how *much* she wanted to go. Torn, she debated with herself, finally deciding she could always e-mail Coach and tell him something had come up. Maybe they could even meet later.

"If you've got plans, that's okay," Nick said.

She shook her head slowly. "No, I don't, not really. All right, I'll meet you at Chuck's at eight."

What are you doing? she asked herself as she drove the short distance home. Just what do you think you're doing? But there was no answer to that question, because Lorna didn't know. All she really knew was that she wanted to go to Chuck's and have a hamburger and beer with Nick. And she didn't want to analyze why, either.

She thought about how Claudia had said she wasn't spontaneous or adventurous. Well, tonight she was going to be both.

Claudia would be proud of her.

Nick whistled as he showered and dressed, fed Maggie and checked his messages. Still nothing from Lorna. It had been interesting to see her debate whether or not to meet him at Chuck's. He'd have given anything to know what she'd been thinking.

It had been a stroke of luck that Nick had seen her leaving work tonight. With her nylon running shorts, T-shirt, sweatband and running shoes, he'd known immediately that she'd planned to run. As soon as he'd realized where she was going, he'd hurriedly changed into his own running gear and hightailed it after her. He'd figured she only had about a five-minute head start, and he'd been right.

He wondered what she would tell Coach about not meeting him online tonight. Nick couldn't help smiling. It was kind of fun to play one persona against the other, even if they were both him.

What wasn't fun was thinking about how she'd react if she ever put two and two together. Or if he ever just came out and told her the truth.

But if or when that day came, it would be far into the future. So why worry about it now?

Lorna couldn't decide what to wear. After tossing aside half a dozen outfits, she thought how silly she was being. This wasn't a date. It was just a friendly hamburger with a co-worker. *Okay, fine, it's not a date, but I still want to look nice.*

She finally settled on black cropped pants, a black-and-white-striped T-shirt with a low scooped neck and black clogs. She took extra-special care with her makeup and her hair, blowing it dry and pulling it back into a low ponytail and tying a black ribbon around it. Inspecting herself in the mirror when she was finished, she decided she would have to do.

Seeing that she had plenty of time—it was only seven-thirty—she sat down at the computer and logged on to her e-mail program. Ten minutes later, she'd sent off an e-mail to Coach saying she was sorry, but something had come up and she couldn't play WordMaker that night after all, at least not early.

I'll check back when I get home. If you're online, maybe we can get in a game. Otherwise, I'll see you another time....

She had thought about telling him she was meeting Nick, then changed her mind, although she'd told Coach about other dates in the past.

This isn't a date!

A date was where a man asked you to go out with him, said "I would like to take you to dinner" or "How about taking in a movie this weekend?" A date was where the man came to your home and picked you up and brought you back afterward.

This was not a date.

This was having a casual meal together, a spur of the moment thing because they'd accidentally met while running.

She was still telling herself to get a grip—this wasn't a date—when she pulled into Chuck's parking lot a few minutes before eight.

As she walked to the door, she spied Nick's pickup. It pleased her that he was already there, that she wouldn't have to wait for him.

When she walked inside the noisy ice house, the first person she saw was Nick walking toward her. Whoa, she thought. He looked amazing in tight jeans and a dark T-shirt that hugged his chest. Amazing and hot. And when he smiled at her, something flipped in her stomach.

"Hey," he said when he reached her. His gaze traveled down, then back up to meet hers. "You sure clean up good."

She grinned. "So do you."

"Come on, I've got us a table outside. Is that okay?"

"Sure." Since the sun had gone down, the temperature had dropped into the eighties, and there was a nice breeze now, so it would be pleasant outside. And a lot less noisy. They wouldn't have to shout to talk.

Their waiter put them at a table by the wrought-iron fence that enclosed the outdoor patio. Several blooming oleanders were planted nearby, and the starlike flowers gave off an intoxicating fragrance. It was a cloudless night with a full moon. A perfect night to be outdoors, Lorna thought as she looked around.

Once they'd placed their orders, Nick said, "Do you normally run every night?"

"Not every night, but I do try to go at least three times a week."

"Yeah, I try to work out regularly, too."

"Oh, I think you do more than try."

"Why do you say that?"

"C'mon, Nick, you don't look as fit as you do without either doing manual labor or working out a lot. And I know you're not doing manual labor."

He smiled. "The same could be said for you."

"Me?"

"Yes, you." The smile expanded, became teasing. "You have a great body."

Lorna was glad it was nighttime, because she knew she was blushing. "No, I don't. I'm too skinny."

"You're not too skinny. In fact, I'd say you're perfect."

Lorna couldn't think of a thing to say in return. No one had ever told her she was perfect before. Ever. Her eyes met Nick's across the table, then—flustered—she looked away. Her heart was beating too fast.

She wished she was more clever with snappy comebacks. She wished she was more sophisticated and experienced with men. She wished her emotions weren't so damned *transparent*.

But mostly, she wished she knew what *he* was thinking. *Don't forget! You cannot afford to lower your guard with this man....*

Because if she allowed herself to believe in him, if she deluded herself into thinking he was interested in her in a romantic way, and then found out otherwise—the way she'd found out Keith's true colors—she would be hurt. And she had a feeling it wouldn't be a minor hurt, but something major and not easy to recover from.

And then what?

She had to work with Nick.

She had to see him every day.

That would be unendurable.

She'd end up having to leave Houston. Or finding another job. Because *he* certainly wouldn't leave.

Just then, their waiter appeared with their order, so Lorna was saved from having to say anything. After he left, Nick busied himself with fixing his hamburger and, to Lorna's great relief, dropped the uncomfortable subject of her body. But she couldn't stop thinking about what Nick had said. And she couldn't help wishing that he really liked her, that his attentions had nothing to do with what she could do for him job-wise, that he sincerely wanted them to be friends.

Friends? Quit lying to yourself. You already want more than that, and you know it.

Afraid her thoughts would show on her face, Lorna turned her attention to her food.

Nick loved watching Lorna eat. Some women picked at their food, either because they didn't really like eating or because they were so paranoid over gaining weight they were afraid to eat.

Lorna ate with obvious enjoyment.

It still amazed him that he'd once thought of her as cold. She was actually one of the warmest women he'd ever known. Warm, smart, funny and beautiful. Just the kind of woman he'd been looking for, he thought ruefully.

If only she was Lorna Smith or Lorna Jones and not Lorna Hathaway. If only she wasn't a dozen rungs up on the social and economic ladder. If only she didn't own the company he worked for.

Yeah, if only I had a million bucks! He figured he was as likely to be granted that wish as any of the others.

"I've been meaning to ask you," he said, forcing his dismal thoughts out of his mind. "Did you ever tell your online buddy what I said about him?"

She laughed. "I did. And guess what *he* said?"

He loved the sound of her laugh—low and throaty and sexy as hell. "What?"

"He said the exact same thing about you! He also asked if I could trust you."

There was a drop of mustard at the corner of her mouth, which she licked off with the tip of her tongue. Nick wanted nothing more than to lean forward and help her, to put his own tongue there and taste what he was sure was the sweetness of her mouth. What would she do if he did? Would she kiss him back? Or would she be shocked?

"And what did *you* say?"

"I said you were very nice and that, yes, I...hoped I could trust you." Her gaze met his. "Can I trust you, Nick?"

"Why *couldn't* you trust me?" he countered.

She shrugged. Dipped a French fry in ketchup. "I don't know. Just...a feeling I have."

He took the last bite of his burger, then wiped his mouth off before answering. "That kind of hurts my feelings, Lorna."

"Really?"

He frowned. "Yes, really."

"There was a time when I wasn't sure if you *had* feelings," she said thoughtfully.

He stared at her. Now his feelings really *were* hurt. "And that's what you really think of me."

"I didn't say that's what I *think*. I said it's what I *used* to think."

"May I ask why?"

"Well, you have to admit that there was a time you went out of your way to be obnoxious to me."

He'd never been obnoxious to her. *Had* he? "When?"

"I can't remember specific incidents. It was just the *way* you talked to me. As if you disliked me."

He wanted to say she was wrong, but down deep he knew she wasn't. Suddenly, he felt like a class A jerk for the way he'd treated her in the past. What the *hell* had been wrong with him? "Lorna…"

"I'm sorry. I shouldn't have said anything."

"No. I'm glad you did. You're right. *I'm* the one who's sorry." He reached across the table, putting his hand over hers. "A while back you asked if we could call a truce. I'll go you one better. Why don't we just start fresh?"

After a long moment, she said, "I'd like that."

"No preconceived ideas about each other."

Now she smiled. "None."

Reluctantly, he released her hand. "Good." He grinned. "In fact, great."

Before she could reply, their waiter approached to clear the table. After that, Nick took care of the bill, and the opportunity to continue their conversation had passed. Probably best, he thought. Because although he'd said they were starting fresh, in his heart he knew that wasn't possible.

They still carried the same baggage. And they always would. The stark reality was, she was still Lorna Hathaway, completely out of his realm.

* * *

Lorna was still a bit unnerved by the turn their conversation had taken. What had possessed her to say those things to him? And yet, maybe it was a good thing she had. After all, she'd only spoken the truth.

As they walked back through the restaurant to the front door, she decided no harm had been done and maybe she'd actually accomplished something good.

"Nicky!"

Lorna looked up. A pretty, dark-haired woman stood grinning at Nick. One of his former girlfriends, no doubt. Lorna immediately disliked her.

"Hello, Marie." Nick looked beyond her. "And Rich. What are you two doing here?"

The woman said, "We come here all the time. It's one of our favorite places." She looked curiously at Lorna. "Hello."

"Lorna," Nick said, drawing her forward, "I'd like you to meet my sister, Marie, and her husband, Rich Fabrizio. Marie, Rich, this is Lorna Hathaway."

Lorna smiled. His sister! "Hi. It's nice to meet you."

"It's nice to meet you, too," Marie said. Her gaze was speculative. "Hathaway. Are you related to the Hathaways who own the company Nick works for?"

Lorna nodded. "Yes. Actually, I work at the Houston plant, too."

"Really? How come you never said anything, Nicky?"

Lorna glanced at Nick. She smothered a smile at the expression on his face.

"Marie…" her husband said.

"Well! He *didn't.*"

"I don't tell you everything," Nick said dryly.

"Obviously. Well, anyway," Marie said, turning back to Lorna, "I'm glad to meet you. How long have you been working at the plant?"

"Just a couple of months."

"Really?"

Lorna could tell Nick's sister was dying to keep asking questions, but her husband took her arm and said, "We're keeping them, Marie."

"Oh. Yeah. Sorry. Well, it was nice meeting you, Lorna." Then she laughed. "I've already said that, haven't I?"

"Only about three times," Nick said. But he was grinning.

Lorna couldn't stop smiling. She liked Nick's sister. And she liked their obviously close relationship.

Once they were outside, Nick said, "Sorry about that."

"What's there to be sorry about?"

"You know. My sister. She's kind of nosy."

"I thought she was sweet."

Nick laughed. "Sweet! That's the first time I've ever heard Marie described as sweet."

"Well, she *was.*"

He just shook his head. "I'll be in for it now, you know."

"What do you mean?"

"She'll tell everybody in my family that she saw us together."

"Is that bad?"

"As long as you don't mind being dinner table conversation at the DeSanto household."

"You don't plan to say anything *bad* about me, do you?"

"No."

"In that case, I don't mind at all."

Chapter Ten

"My truck's there," Lorna said, pointing to the opposite end of the parking lot.

"I'll walk you over." For a moment, Nick thought she was going to protest, but she didn't.

As they approached the SUV, she dug into her handbag and pulled out her keys, unlocking it with her remote. Without conscious thought, he moved closer, so that when she stopped and turned to say goodbye, they were standing only inches apart.

Neither moved as a gust of wind rattled the leaves of a nearby aspen tree. Her eyes met his and something stirred in the air between them.

Nick wanted to kiss her.

He wanted to kiss her more than he'd wanted anything in a long time.

He knew kissing her was a bad idea.

He knew if he did, he would probably be sorry. Then, just as he decided he didn't care, he was going to kiss her and damn the consequences, a phone rang.

She jumped. "It's mine." Pulling the cell phone out of her handbag, she pressed a button and said hello. *Sorry,* she mouthed.

Taking a deep breath, Nick moved slightly away and leaned against her truck. Close call, he thought. Too damn close. *What the hell are you playing with, DeSanto?* But the desire to kiss her was still there.

Lorna listened to whoever had called her for a few seconds, then exclaimed, "Oh, no! What happened? Are they all right?"

Nick stiffened.

"Oh, God. I—I'll be right there. Where, exactly, are you?" She looked stricken.

"What is it?" Nick said when she'd disconnected the call.

He could see she was fighting tears. "M-my sister, Claudia, she and her husband have been in an automobile accident, and they've been taken to Mercy Hospital. She might lose her...baby." This last was said around a sob. "I—I have to go to her."

"I'll drive you."

"No, you don't have to do that. I—I can drive myself."

"I'm driving you." Taking her keys from her lifeless fingers, he locked her truck, then took her hand and led her across the asphalt to where his truck was parked. Opening the passenger side door, he helped her inside, ignoring her continued protests, because he could see she wasn't in any shape to drive anywhere. Hell, she'd probably have an accident herself!

It was a lucky thing the call had come when it had. A few minutes later, and she'd have already been on the road. Now he could see that she got to the hospital safely.

"I—I'd better call my brother," she said.

He listened as she talked, knowing from what she said that she wasn't able to raise Bryce and was leaving him a message. When she disconnected the call, she bowed her head. Her shoulders shook, and he knew she was crying.

He reached across the seat, putting his hand on her arm. "Lorna…"

"I'm sorry," she gulped.

"It's okay to be scared. I know how you feel." And he did. He remembered how worried he and everyone else in his family had been when they were afraid Marie had cervical cancer a few years back. The twenty-four hours they'd waited for the lab report had been agony.

"It's just that—" She stopped.

"What?" he asked gently.

"I—" She swallowed. "I was so envious when she told me she was pregnant."

"Hey. This accident isn't your fault, if that's what you're thinking." He flipped on his right turn signal.

She sniffed. "Oh, I know. I just pray nothing happens. Claudia will be devastated if she loses the baby."

"They've got great doctors down at Mercy. If there's any way to save the baby, they'll do it."

She took a deep breath. Made a valiant attempt to smile. Tears still glistened in her eyes, and she looked more vulnerable than he'd ever imagined. Suddenly all he wanted was the right to pull her into his arms. In that moment, Nick knew he was a goner. He might never be successful in winning Lorna's love, but he promised himself that no matter what it took, he was going to give it his best shot.

Lorna was so grateful Nick hadn't listened to her when she'd told him she could drive herself. It was such a relief to have him there to reassure her, to have him take charge, to find a place to park, to hold her hand as they raced through the garage into the hospital, to find out exactly where they needed to go and how to get there once they were inside.

After being told that Claudia and John were still in the E.R., they quickly headed in that direction. Entering the waiting area, Lorna immediately spied John's sister Jennifer standing by one of the windows.

"Jennifer," she called.

Jennifer whirled around. Her face reflected the strain she was under. "Oh, Lorna, I'm so glad you're here. We've been so worried."

It was only then that Lorna realized Jennifer wasn't alone. Having met John's family at his and Claudia's wedding, she recognized Philip Larkin, Jennifer's cousin and the man who had also been in love with Claudia, as he stepped forward to greet them.

Lorna introduced the two of them to Nick, saying, "Nick and I work together and he was with me when I got your call."

Nick shook hands with both John's sister and his cousin.

"My parents would be here, too," Jennifer said, "but they're in Hawaii on vacation. I didn't even call them because I knew they'd just worry, and they can't do anything." Her own forehead creased with worry. "Do you think I did the right thing?"

"Absolutely," Lorna said. "I'm not calling my mother, either. She's in Europe right now."

Nick was proud of Lorna for conquering her *own* fear long enough to comfort Jennifer.

"Where are Claudia and John?" Lorna asked. "What's happened since we talked?"

"John is having his ribs taped. It looks like his seat

belt jerked him back so hard, he cracked a couple of them in the process. And right now they're doing an ultrasound on Claudia. The doctor told me that normally they don't worry, because the fetus is well protected by the amniotic fluid, even in an accident, but apparently the baby's heartbeat is irregular, and this *does* worry them."

Lorna put her hand over her mouth, and Nick wished again he could draw her close.

"The doctor also said that if she *does* miscarry, it probably won't have anything to do with the accident. That more than likely, there's some abnormality that would have caused it, anyway."

Lorna nodded distractedly. "When will they know?"

Jennifer shook her head. "I don't know. We'll just have to wait."

After that, the four of them sat without talking. Nick watched Lorna, who stared into space. He wondered what she was thinking. Remembering what she'd said on the way over, how she'd been so envious of Claudia, he wondered if she was still—in some odd way—blaming herself. He hoped not. For the first time since he'd known her, he wondered why she and her ex-husband hadn't had any children. Funny. That was one subject she and Coach hadn't ever talked about, other than to say they were both childless.

Now he wondered. Couldn't she *have* children?

And if she couldn't…would that make any difference to him? He didn't have to think about the question for very long. He knew the answer. No. It wouldn't make any difference. Yes, he wanted children, but if he were lucky enough to win Lorna, they could adopt. Hell, there were thousands of unwanted kids out there, and any one of them would be lucky to have her as a mother.

He was still thinking about Lorna and all the things he wanted to learn about her when, close to an hour later, a harried-looking doctor came out to talk to them.

"I'm going to move Mrs. Renzo from the E.R. into a room. She's okay, and for now, the baby's stabilized, but we're still not sure she won't miscarry. We think it's best if she stays here a couple of days, just to be on the safe side. That way we can keep a close watch on her."

"What about my brother?" Jennifer asked.

"He's being released."

"Can I see him?"

"As soon as he signs some papers, he'll be out."

When John Renzo, walking gingerly, joined them fifteen minutes later, Nick began to feel like a fifth wheel. Although he'd have liked to stay with Lorna, he knew he didn't belong in this family circle. Not yet, anyway.

So once they'd all decided they were going to the

fourth floor, which is where Claudia would be moved, Nick pulled Lorna aside. "Listen, I've been thinking," he said. "Why don't you give me your keys, and I'll drive over to Chuck's and pick up your truck and bring it back here for you."

"But what will *you* do without your truck?"

"I'll take a cab back to Chuck's."

"No, Nick, you don't have to do that. I can get a ride back to the restaurant later."

"I want to."

"But—"

"Let me do this for you, Lorna."

There must have been something in his expression that told her how much he wanted to be able to help out, because she slowly smiled. "Thank you, Nick," she said softly. "Thank you for everything."

"Anytime," he said with an answering smile.

She dug in her handbag and produced her keys.

He took them, and their fingertips brushed. His eyes met hers. "I'll be back in about thirty minutes," he said. And then, before he could talk himself out of it, he bent down and kissed her lightly on the lips.

Bryce and Amy arrived at the hospital at three-thirty in the morning. Tears in their eyes, Amy and Lorna hugged. Then Bryce drew Lorna close.

"It's going to be okay," he said.

Even though Lorna nodded, she knew neither of

them could predict what would happen. Only time would tell.

Please, God, she prayed, *please let the baby make it.* This was the same prayer she'd whispered ever since she'd gotten the news of the accident.

"Chloe wanted to come, too," Bryce said. "But she couldn't leave Cameron alone. Greg's in Boston on business."

Lorna didn't say what she was thinking, that Chloe could have brought Cameron with her. Oh, well. Long ago she'd decided Chloe was more like their mother than was good for her, but that was not Lorna's problem. Right now, all she really cared about was Claudia and her baby.

"Tell us everything," Amy said. Her expression told Lorna she knew exactly what Lorna had been thinking.

So Lorna brought them up to date on Claudia's condition and what the doctor had told them. Then Amy asked if they could go in to see Claudia.

"You can peek in on her," Lorna said. "They gave her something to make her sleep."

"Where's John?" Bryce said.

"He's in the room with her. They set up a cot for him because he refused to leave her. They gave him something for pain, too, and that should help him sleep."

"What about his family?"

"Jennifer and his cousin went down to the cafeteria for some coffee. His parents are in Hawaii on vacation." Lorna frowned. "Do you think I should have called Mother?"

Bryce shrugged. "I don't see what good it would do. Besides, I'm not even sure where they are now. Maybe en route to Greece."

"Has Claudia asked about her?" Amy asked.

Lorna shook her head. That was pretty sad, she knew, but Claudia, like the rest of them, had gotten used to not depending on their mother for anything. Lorna doubted that would change, even if their mother should.

They talked awhile longer, then Lorna took them to Claudia's room. She didn't go in with them; she'd already seen Claudia. A few minutes later, Bryce and Amy came out.

"Was she awake?" Lorna asked.

Bryce shook his head. "She sure is banged up. Didn't she have her seat belt on?"

"Yes, but apparently she didn't have her contacts in and the force of the air bag slamming against her glasses is what caused the facial bruising. Plus the truck rolled, so she was really shaken up." Lorna shuddered every time she thought about the truck rolling. Thank God for the air bags.

They continued to talk about the accident, with Lorna explaining where it had happened and all the details she knew. She also reiterated what the doctor had said about the accident not being the cause of a possible miscarriage. After that, they sat quietly, not saying much. Amy fell asleep, and even Bryce nodded off, but Lorna was still wide-awake—too keyed up and too worried to sleep. Of course, she didn't have four small children to run her ragged every day, either, like Bryce and Amy did.

When the first pale pink of dawn lightened the windows, the hospital began to stir again. The morning shift of nurses appeared, their rubber-soled shoes soundless on the tile floors. An aide walked off the elevator pushing the breakfast meal cart for the wing. The metal covers clanged as she maneuvered it into place across from the nurses' station.

Bryce stretched and yawned. He glanced down at his watch, then over at Amy, who was now curled up on the leather couch, her sweater balled up under her head as a pillow. He smiled.

Lorna felt a pang as she watched the way he looked at his wife. She wanted someone to look at her like that. *Someone.* Not just someone, she thought. *Be honest.* She swallowed. The truth was, she wanted Nick to look at her that way. *Oh, God, I'm so stupid. Will I ever learn? Will I ever stop being attracted to the wrong man?*

For about the hundredth time since he'd left her

the night before, she remembered how he'd kissed her. She had to force herself not to touch her lips.

It hadn't been much of a kiss. Almost the kind you'd give any friend when you said goodbye.

But they weren't that kind of friends.

Were they?

So what had the kiss meant?

She wished she had someone to ask. She had almost told Amy about the kiss, but then she'd decided not to. If their relationship didn't progress any further, she'd rather not have anyone know what she'd hoped.

I'll just have to figure this one out myself.

After a breakfast of black coffee and a toasted bagel, Nick called Mercy Hospital to check on Claudia. He'd have liked to call Lorna, but if she was at home, she was probably asleep, and if she was still at the hospital—which was probably the case—her cell phone wouldn't be accessible. Besides, she'd promised to call him when she had anything to report.

"There's no change in Mrs. Renzo's condition," the information operator said.

"Is there a phone in her room?" Nick asked.

"No calls are being put through."

Nick debated what to do after hanging up. If Lorna *was* still there, he hoped she was doing okay. Knowing there was only one way to be sure, he decided to go to the hospital to check on her.

When he arrived, he headed straight up to the fourth floor. As he exited the elevator, he almost collided with Bryce Hathaway.

"Nick! What are *you* doing here?" Bryce said.

"I just came by to check on Lorna, make sure she was okay."

"How'd you know Lorna was here?"

"She and I had dinner together last night, and I was with her when she got the call from Jennifer Renzo. I brought her to the hospital. She didn't tell you?"

"No."

Nick could see the curiosity in Bryce's eyes. "She was pretty shook up. I didn't think she should drive herself."

"That was good of you."

"So how's Claudia doing?"

"She's fine. They're still worried about the baby, though. They're talking about complete bed rest for her until she's out of the woods."

"Here, you mean?"

"No. Once they're sure the pregnancy is stabilized, they'll allow her to go home. But she might not be able to go back to work." Bryce grimaced. "That'll kill her. She's not the type to sit around."

"How's John doing today?"

"He's okay. Sore and on pain pills because of those ribs, but nothing serious."

"That's good."

"Yeah, it is." Bryce shook his head. "It was a bad accident."

"Yeah, John told us what happened last night."

"They were damned lucky," Bryce said.

Nick nodded, remembering John's description of the accident. He and Claudia were on their way home, driving west on the Katy Freeway where it merges with the 610 Loop and were cut off by a car that wanted to exit to the Loop but was in the wrong lane. In trying to avoid hitting the other car, John lost control of his truck and they smashed into a concrete barrier, then rolled over and were hit from behind.

"Well," Bryce said, "I'm on my way downstairs to get some breakfast. Amy and Lorna just got back from having theirs. They're in seeing Claudia now. Did you want to see her?"

Nick shook his head. "No, I'll wait out here. I just wanted to check on Lorna. Make sure she was doing okay."

Again, Bryce gave him a curious look, but he didn't say anything. After Bryce got on the elevator, Nick walked to the waiting area and sat down. About ten minutes later, the door to one of the rooms opened, and Lorna and Amy walked out. At first they didn't see him; they were too busy talking. Then Amy looked up. Her eyes widened, and she nudged Lorna.

Lorna seemed taken aback, and it was a moment

before she smiled in welcome. He wondered what she was thinking. If she was remembering, as he was, the way he'd kissed her goodbye last night.

It was obvious she hadn't been home, because she was still dressed in the outfit she'd worn to dinner the night before. As she came closer, he could see how tired she looked. No wonder. It couldn't have been fun to spend the night there. Amy, too, looked tired. But both women had happy smiles on their faces as they greeted him.

"I saw Bryce when I got off the elevator," Nick said. "He told me Claudia's doing much better."

"Yes," Lorna said. "In fact, her doctor's in with her now, and they're thinking they may release her this afternoon." The relief on her face was palpable.

"That's great news." Turning to Amy, he said, "It's good to see you again, Amy."

"You, too, Nick." Like her husband, she couldn't disguise her curiosity.

What the hell, he thought. Go for broke. "I was worried about you," he said to Lorna.

She blushed. "I—I'm fine."

"Are you sure? You look exhausted." He could feel Amy's sharp eyes watching them.

"I didn't sleep much."

"Are you going to stay here all day today?"

"Yes, until Claudia's released."

"What if they don't let her go today?"

She shrugged. "I don't know. I'll probably go home to shower and change clothes, then come back."

Realizing Jennifer Renzo and Philip Larkin were nowhere to be seen, he said, "What happened to John's sister?"

"They went home last night and are planning to come back later today."

"You should probably get some sleep, too."

"I'll be okay."

During this entire exchange, Amy hadn't said a word. Now she spoke up. "I've been trying to talk her into going home, but she's stubborn."

Nick smiled. "Yes, I know."

"You're just as tired as I am," Lorna said to Amy. "Why don't *you* go to the house?"

"I slept almost all night," Amy said. "First in the car, then here. You and Bryce are the ones who need to get some sleep."

Nick shook his head. "I can see we're going to go nowhere with this discussion."

Amy nodded.

"Okay," Nick continued, "how about this? Why don't I take you home, Lorna? You can have a quick shower and change clothes, then I'll bring you back."

"Yes, Lorna," Amy urged. "Go. You'll feel a lot better if you do."

"Only if you promise to do the same when I get back," Lorna said.

Amy grinned. "It's a deal."

"But I can drive myself," Lorna said to Nick. "I'm sure you have things to do."

"Would I have offered if I had things to do?" he countered. "Besides, it'll be easier for both of you. When we get back, I'll drop you off and take Amy."

When Lorna finally agreed and turned her back to get her purse, Amy winked at Nick.

Nick grinned. He had the distinct feeling she saw right through him. But that was okay. Because he also had a feeling she was on his side.

Chapter Eleven

In the end, Claudia's doctors decided to keep her one more night. Both she and John urged their families to go home and get a good night's sleep.

"She's no longer in danger of losing the baby," John said, "so there's no reason to subject yourself to any more torture."

"It's not torture to stay here with you," his sister protested, looking to Lorna for help.

"I agree," Lorna said, although she dreaded another night spent on a chair.

"You're going home," John insisted. "I've still got

a cot in her room. Believe me, I'll call you if anything happens, but nothing's going to."

"Please, Lorna, listen to John," Claudia said from her bed. "And Bryce, you and Amy definitely need to get a good night's sleep if you're driving back to Morgan Creek tomorrow."

"I wish we could stay longer," Amy said, "but I only left enough breast milk to last through tomorrow morning, and Emily isn't going to be happy if I'm not there to feed her once that's gone."

Lorna knew it had been hard for Amy to leave her baby. After all, Emily was barely four months old. Amy was lucky, though. Mrs. Janney, the Hathaway housekeeper and Lucy, a trusted maid who had a toddler of her own, were competent to take care of the girls while Bryce and Amy were away.

"Then it's settled," Claudia said. "You're all going to sleep in your own beds tonight."

Lorna kissed Claudia goodbye, told her she'd be there in the morning to help John get her home safely, then headed out to the lounge area where Nick was waiting. It still amazed her that he'd stayed at the hospital all day.

What did his attentions mean?

Was he here to impress Bryce?

Or was he here because of her?

She was afraid to hope.

A few seconds later, Amy and Bryce joined them.

Bryce said, "If you haven't got anything else scheduled, why don't you join us for dinner, Nick?"

Lorna glanced over at Nick. He probably had a date. After all, it *was* Saturday night. Her heart beat faster as she waited for his answer.

"Thanks, I'd like that," Nick said. "Where are you planning to go?"

"I don't know. We hadn't talked about it. What do you think, Lorna?"

"I'm too tired to go anywhere. I was hoping we could just pick up something and take it to my house."

"That's a great idea," Amy said. "I'm exhausted myself. It'll be good to just crash."

After a few more minutes of discussion, they decided on Thai takeout, which Nick offered to stop and get on the way to Lorna's.

"I'll ride along with you," Bryce said. "Amy can go with Lorna."

Lorna was glad Bryce had suggested this arrangement. She wouldn't have wanted Nick to pay for the food, and she was sure Bryce wouldn't allow him to.

Bryce transferred Amy's overnight bag to Lorna's truck, and then he and Nick took off.

After reaching Lorna's, Amy took the first shower. By the time Lorna took her shower and had changed into a clean blue T-shirt and jeans, she could hear the men in the kitchen.

"Here she is," Amy said when Lorna joined them. "We were just looking for napkins."

Lorna made a face. "I forgot to put them on my grocery list. We'll have to use paper towels."

"Hey, it'll seem like home," Nick joked.

"This is sure better than hospital cafeteria food," Bryce said with an appreciative sniff as the aromas of the different dishes began to permeate the kitchen.

"It's better than anything we can get in Morgan Creek, too," Amy commented.

"Yes," Lorna agreed, "that's one of the real benefits of living in Houston. We have fantastic restaurants."

"Listen to her," Bryce said. "It's *we* already."

Lorna laughed. "I do feel at home here." She glanced over at Nick, who was helping himself to Thai curry chicken. "You were born here, weren't you, Nick?"

"Yep, born and bred, although for a while, I lived in Dallas."

"Did you like it there?"

"I like Houston better."

Lorna grinned. "I hadn't lived here one week when I realized what a huge rivalry there is between Houston and Dallas, at least on the part of Houstonians."

"We're still smarting over 'America's Team,'" Nick said dryly.

"That *was* pretty cheeky on their part," Bryce said, laughing.

"Why'd you move to Dallas, Nick?" This came from Amy.

"Oh, you know how it is when you're young. You want to get as far away from your family as you can. Besides, my best job offer came from a Dallas-based company."

"But you're close to your family now," Lorna pointed out.

"What can I say? I grew up." He grinned. "It takes some of us longer than others. Now I realize how important my family is to me."

She loved that he wasn't shy about admitting his feelings. In that respect, he reminded her of Coach. Suddenly, her eyes widened and she involuntarily gasped.

"What is it?" Amy said, frowning.

"Oh, nothing. I—I just remembered something I forgot to do." God. Lorna couldn't believe she hadn't thought of Coach once since she'd gotten the call about Claudia Friday night. She knew he was probably worried about her and wondering what had happened to her. Well, it couldn't be helped. And she certainly couldn't excuse herself now and go back to her computer. Writing him would just have to wait until Nick, at least, was gone.

"Something important?" Amy pressed.

"Just an appointment I had."

"Oh, dear. Do you want to call now and explain what happened?"

Lorna wished Amy wasn't so nice. She didn't like lying to her sister-in-law, but she didn't have a choice. "No, it's okay. I can…call tomorrow. It's not a problem. I just couldn't believe I forgot." Hoping the subject would be dropped, she squeezed some lime on her Pad Thai, then took a big bite. "Umm, this is so good." As she looked up, her gaze collided with Nick's. Something about the way he was studying her made her feel uncomfortable, almost as if he knew that she hadn't been telling them the truth about the forgotten appointment.

Oh, you're paranoid. You think everyone knows when you're fibbing.

"So Nick," Amy said, "how many are in your family?"

"I have two brothers and a sister and their spouses and assorted nieces and nephews, uncles, aunts and cousins. And, of course, my parents."

"And they all live in Houston?"

"Yes."

"You're lucky," Amy said wistfully. "I've been trying to talk my dad into moving to Morgan Creek, but so far, no luck."

"He lives in Florida, right?" Nick said.

Amy smiled. "I can't believe you remembered!

And yes, he lives in Florida. The trouble is, as much as he loves me and his granddaughters, he's in his eighties now, and it's hard to leave the place you've lived all your life. All his friends are there, and I guess he figures he'd be a burden to us if he moved to Morgan Creek." She sighed. "All I can do is keep trying to convince him, I guess."

"You don't have any brothers and sisters?"

"No." Then she turned her brown-eyed gaze to Lorna. "But I have wonderful sisters-in-law."

Lorna reached over and squeezed Amy's hand. "And we all love you."

For a few minutes, they ate quietly. Lorna had produced a bottle of Pinot Grigio and the combination of good food and good wine relaxed her enough that she stopped questioning why Nick was there and just enjoyed his company. She still couldn't get over how different he had turned out to be from what she'd originally thought. In fact, she admitted ruefully, he was exactly the kind of man she'd always dreamed of finding.

"Nick," Bryce said toward the end of their meal, "have you done any work on an expansion proposal yet?"

Nick shook his head. "I thought Lorna and I could put our heads together in the next couple of weeks and come up with a plan."

Lorna blinked. He intended to include *her* in the

planning stages? She remembered how he'd once told her what her job entailed. Management-level planning hadn't been included. What had brought about *that* change in his thinking? Oh, how she wished she could believe he wanted her there because of her knowledge and experience and not because he thought he'd score points with Bryce or have a better chance of getting his proposal through if she had played a major part in the planning.

Are you being fair?

She probably wasn't. Unfortunately, she was doomed to suspect the motives of any man who showed an interest in her. And who could blame her? With her background, it was impossible not to wonder what attracted them—her, her money, or the family name. And Nick was no exception. In fact, Nick probably had even more reason to court her favor than someone who *wasn't* affiliated with the company.

Coach is the only man you know who isn't suspect.

Because Coach didn't know she was rich. Coach liked her for who she was inside, not for what she possessed in terms of wealth or position.

She glanced at Nick, who was talking animatedly to Bryce. She wanted to believe in him so badly. And yet, no matter how much she wanted to think he was sincere in his attentions to her, she knew it would be foolish to ignore her past experiences.

Some of her pleasure in the day faded. And when

Nick said he ought to be taking off so that they could get some much needed rest, she didn't try to persuade him otherwise. She did walk him to the front door and thanked him for everything he'd done for her over the weekend.

"I'm just glad I could help," he said.

Looking into his dark eyes and seeing a concern she would have sworn wasn't fake, she was sorry about her earlier negative thoughts. But her fear of getting hurt was stronger than her need to believe in him, so she kept her voice light when she answered. "Well, thanks again. I'll see you Monday."

He nodded, his gaze still locked with hers.

For a moment, she thought he was going to kiss her again, and if he did, she knew she wouldn't have the willpower to keep from kissing him back. From somewhere she found the strength to tear her gaze from his, to back away and smile a casual goodbye.

When she closed the door behind him, she had to take several deep breaths to calm herself before she could face Bryce and Amy again.

Nick almost called his mother to say he couldn't make dinner Sunday afternoon because he wasn't looking forward to getting the third degree. But he knew that whether or not he went to his parents' house, his sister would have plenty to say about what she'd seen Friday night. Better to be there, he decided. That way he might be able to deflect some of her curiosity.

Sure enough, the family had barely sat down to dinner when Marie started.

"So Nicky," she said, "tell us about Lorna Hathaway."

He looked over at her with what he hoped was a bland expression. "What would you like to know?"

"For starters, when did you start dating her?"

"Lorna Hathaway," his mother said thoughtfully as she passed the mashed potatoes. "Is she related to the people who own your company?"

"Yes, Ma. She *is* one of the owners," Nick said. He turned back to his sister. "I'm not dating her, Marie."

"Oh, come on, Nick. I'm not stupid, you know." Marie looked at her mother. "We saw the two of them on Friday night. And it was definitely a date. Don't let him kid you."

"It wasn't a date," he said more firmly, trying not to get mad, for that would just encourage Marie all the more. "It was just two co-workers having dinner together." He took a helping of roast pork and passed the platter to his sister-in-law Kathy.

"Hah!" Marie grinned. "Just two co-workers having dinner together," she mimicked.

Boy, he'd like to strangle her.

"Is she single?" His mother's eyes were bright.

"She's divorced," Nick said.

His mother nodded again.

Oh, man, he could see the wheels turning. He ate some of his butternut squash. "Good squash, Mom," he said, hoping to steer her away from the subject of Lorna.

No such luck.

"Thank you. Does she have children?" she asked.

He sighed inwardly. "No, Ma, she doesn't have any children."

"What does she look like, Marie?" Jay asked.

Hell. Were they *all* going to latch on to this topic now?

"She's pretty," Marie conceded. "Tall and blonde. Kind of skinny, though. But she seemed nice."

Nick almost said, *she's not skinny*, then thought better of it. That's all he needed to do, start defending Lorna. Then they'd *never* give him any peace.

"So why *aren't* you dating her, Nick?" Mike asked around a mouthful of potatoes. "If she's tall, blond, pretty and rich—hell, she sounds perfect." He laughed at his own joke and nudged his wife Candy, who rolled her eyes.

Nick just looked at his brother. "Do I have to spell it out? She's a Hathaway, that's why."

"So?" he said.

"So it should be obvious why we're not dating. I'm hardly in her class."

"Why would you *say* such a thing?" his mother

said indignantly. "You're good enough for *anyone*. Why, any girl would be *lucky* to get you."

Nick grinned. "Hey, Ma, you're a little bit prejudiced, don't you think?"

"I am not! I'm only speaking the truth."

"Yeah, Nick," Jay said. "So what if she's a Hathaway? Big deal."

"Yeah, Nick," Marie chimed in. "This isn't the dark ages. We're as good as anybody. Right, Pop?"

"And better than most," his father said with a grin.

Jay was wrong. It was a big deal, no matter what his loyal family had to say about it, Nick thought. "Look, can we drop this subject? I don't even *want* to date Lorna Hathaway, so it doesn't matter whether I'm good enough for her or not. Okay?" He hoped he sounded convincing. He hoped they'd move on to something else. He hoped his nose didn't suddenly grow longer.

"Why were you having dinner with her, then?" Marie said. "You can't tell me you were discussing *business* on a Friday night. At Chuck's," she added for emphasis.

"You were at *Chuck's?*" Jay said.

"Jay," Kathy said, "who Nick sees and where he goes is really his own business, you know."

"No one had a problem with sticking their nose into *my* business when *we* started dating," Jay countered.

Kathy gave Nick a sympathetic smile, as if to say, *I tried.*

"Yeah," Marie said, "me and Mike didn't get a break, either, so now it's your turn, Nicky, whether you like it or not."

Sometimes Nick's family drove him bonkers. "Okay, here's what happened. I was jogging at Memorial Park and I ran into Lorna, who was also jogging. We got to talking and decided to meet for a hamburger and continue our discussion. That's it."

"Oh," his mother said.

"Well," Marie said, "I don't believe it for a minute. I saw the way you two were looking at each other."

It was a good thing his sister didn't know how he'd spent the major part of Friday night and yesterday sitting with Lorna at Mercy Hospital. Or how he'd felt when she'd cried in his truck. Or how he couldn't resist kissing her. Or how hard it had been for him to stop himself from kissing her again yesterday. Because if she did know all those things, she'd give him no rest until he admitted the truth. And there was no way, no way in *hell* he'd ever admit to any one of his family how he really felt about Lorna. Because if he did, and then things didn't work out the way he hoped—which there was a good chance they wouldn't—they'd all feel sorry for him.

No. No way. "Can we please change the subject now?" he said.

"I happen to like this subject," Marie said, but

there was no bite in her words, and soon after the talk moved on to Kathy's upcoming exam to become a certified registered nurse anesthetist.

Later, when dinner was over and the women were in the kitchen gabbing, and Nick was sitting in the family room watching the Texans game on TV with his father and brothers, he found his attention wandering.

He kept wondering how Lorna was doing today. He knew Bryce and Amy had been planning to drive back to Morgan Creek this morning. He'd bet Lorna had gone down to the hospital. Maybe she was still there. Probably not, though, since Claudia was supposed to be sent home early.

If her family crisis was over, Lorna would finally contact Coach. Nick felt certain that's what she'd been thinking about at dinner yesterday when she said she'd had an appointment she'd forgotten. Up until then, he hadn't thought about Coach, either, but when she'd said that about the appointment, he'd belatedly realized Coach would have been worried when he didn't hear from her all weekend. So last night after getting home Nick had sent off an e-mail to Sweet Stuff.

Nick was no longer sure how he felt about this whole Coach thing. He couldn't figure out if it would help his case or hinder it for her to find out he was Coach. Trouble was, he felt like he was making progress with her. And now he was worried that revealing his online persona would upset her. Maybe she wouldn't understand why he hadn't revealed his identity as soon as he knew who she was.

Damn. He'd thought he was doing the right thing. Not that it mattered now, because it was too late to change things. He would just have to hope finding out who Coach was wouldn't jinx his chances with her for good.

The first thing Nick did when he got home that evening was check his e-mail. He watched as a message from Lorna downloaded.

From: SweetStuff@jamboree.net
To: Coach1012@bayoucity.net
Subject: An Apology
Dear Coach,
I'm so sorry not to have written to you before this. I hope you weren't waiting for me online Friday night. It's a long story, but here's what happened.

Nick scanned the part where she told about running into him in Memorial Park, then meeting him for dinner and getting the phone call about Claudia. His gaze fastened on the last paragraph.

I've had a lot of time to think in the past few days, and I've realized just how much I've come to value your friendship. You know more about me than anyone except maybe my sister, and you still like me. <g> That means a lot to me. I can't explain, but if you knew my background, you'd understand that in many of my relationships, I haven't been valued for myself but for what the other person thought they might gain out of it. Because of this, it's been hard for me to trust people. But you're different, Coach. I feel I could trust you with my life, that no matter what I might tell you about myself, it wouldn't matter to you, that you would still be my friend.

Anyway, I just wanted you to know that.

What had been going through her mind when she wrote all this? Nick wondered. He leaned back in his chair and stared at the message for a long time. Of course, he knew exactly what she meant about her background and finding it hard to trust people. In her shoes, he'd have felt the same way. He was sure she'd had people try to take advantage of her her entire life.

She'd been thinking about *him* when she wrote that, hadn't she? She'd been questioning *his* motives.

Hell, of course. That was it. That's why she'd seemed to back off last night when he was leaving her house. She'd remembered Coach while they were eating and in remembering had started thinking about how he liked her for herself and how Nick probably wanted something from her.

The question was, what should he do about this?

From: Coach1012@bayoucity.net
To: SweetStuff@jamboree.net
Subject: Re: An Apology
I was really sorry to hear about your sister, but I'm sure glad to know she's okay now. I know you're relieved. I hope you weren't worrying about not letting me know sooner. I figured something important had happened.

Your friendship means a lot to me, too. In fact, I've been thinking about something for a while. I think it's past time for us to try to meet again. What do you think? Want to give it another shot?

Lorna stared at the message for a long time. Her heart was beating too fast, almost as if she thought Coach could see her.

Meet.

He wanted to meet again.

Why now? she wondered. What was different now?

Earlier today, when she'd sent him an e-mail explaining what had happened over the weekend, she would have said she wanted to meet him. Tonight, though, she was once more riddled with doubt.

She had to face it. Yes, he was her friend. And yes,

she trusted him. And yes, she valued his friendship. But despite all that, she wasn't sure she wanted to meet him.

Since the last time they'd set up a meeting, everything had changed.

The trouble was, no matter how she tried to deny it to herself, she was afraid it was too late for her and Coach, because she had fallen in love with Nick.

And her love was hopeless. For even though he'd kissed her, and even though he'd been paying a lot of attention to her, he didn't love her. They'd never even had a real date!

With a heavy heart, she began to write back to Coach.

I need some time to think about meeting. Is that okay? I'm sorry to put you off, but there are some things I need to figure out first.

Between now and the time Coach answered her back, she knew she'd better decide what she was going to do when she could no longer stall for time.

Well, that was promising, Nick thought as he read Lorna's reply to his question about meeting. Maybe he had a better chance with her than he'd thought. Maybe she was stalling for time because of him. He wrote her back immediately.

If you need some time, that's okay. But I hope you don't take too long to decide about us meeting, because I have a feeling we'd really be good together. Don't laugh, but I've had fantasies about you. In my mind, you're the woman of my dreams. I think I've fallen in love with you, Sweet Stuff. I know I shouldn't put you on the spot like this, but I can't help it. I want to meet you in person more than I've wanted anything in a long time.

I think I've fallen in love with you... In my mind you're the woman of my dreams... I've had fantasies about you....

Lorna couldn't fall asleep. Round and round her mind went. Over and over she thought about what he'd said.

When she finally did fall asleep long after midnight, she had an erotic dream about Coach and, like the last time he'd invaded her dreams, he looked and sounded a lot like Nick.

In this dream, the two of them were on a private beach somewhere. The dream was so vivid, Lorna could feel the sun blazing down on them, she could smell the suntan lotion they were wearing, feel the breeze of the palm trees as they swayed overhead, and hear the rush of the water as the waves broke a dozen feet away.

And when he pushed the top of her bikini down and lowered his head to her breasts, and at the same time slipped a hand under the bottom of her suit to find the place that ached for his touch, she cried out.

Her cry woke her, and for a long time afterward, she lay awake. It didn't take a genius to figure out what the dream had meant or what Lorna wanted.

Unfortunately, what she wanted and what would actually happen were two distinctly different things.

Chapter Twelve

For the next week, Lorna avoided Nick as much as possible. Seeing him would only cloud her mind, and she needed to think clearly.

She couldn't stop thinking about what Coach had written. *I think I've fallen in love with you, Sweet Stuff.* What was she going to do? How could she, in good conscience, meet Coach when she felt the way she did about Nick?

She couldn't.

It wouldn't be fair to Coach.

And yet…was she being fair to *herself*?

Maybe Coach was everything she'd imagined. And he loved her. Nick didn't.

We've never even had a real date.

She kept reminding herself of this incontrovertible fact. *You've fallen in love with someone who has only shown you friendship, and a suspect friendship at that.* Another incontrovertible fact.

By the end of the week, Lorna was a wreck. She knew she had to get away. Had to stop thinking about Coach versus Nick or she was going to go crazy.

So at noon on Friday, she walked into Karen's office. Smiling at the younger woman, she said, "Is Nick around?"

"Sorry, he just went to lunch with Cal Lopez."

"Oh." But that was good, Lorna realized. Now she could get away without having to see him. "Would you give him a message for me?"

"Sure."

"Tell him I left early because I'm going to Morgan Creek for the weekend." Lorna didn't feel guilty about taking off before quitting time because she'd already put in more than forty hours this week. And she knew Nick was aware that Claudia was in Morgan Creek and would be for a few weeks of R and R. He would understand that Lorna wanted to be with her after last week's scare.

She felt as if a huge load had been lifted from her shoulders once she was on the road. She ignored the little voice inside that said she was running away.

You do that well, the voice continued. *When things get rough, you don't get tough, you escape....*

"Oh, that's not true!" she muttered. "When have I *ever* run away from a problem?"

You left Florida State when Keith dumped you. You couldn't run fast enough.

"Keith did not dump me. I dumped him."

Whatever.

"Well, I *did.*"

Suddenly Lorna began to laugh. If anyone could hear her talking to herself, they really *would* think she was crazy. Maybe she should save the talking until she could get Amy's and Claudia's opinions.

She had decided she would tell them everything. Even how she felt about Nick.

That decided, she sang along with her favorite CDs for the rest of the way to Morgan Creek and tried not to think of Nick at all.

"If it were me, I'd just lay all my cards on the table. Come right out and tell Nick what Coach said and ask if he thought you should go."

Lorna looked at Claudia. The sisters were sitting in Amy's kitchen and watching Amy roll out piecrust. "You mean the way you did with John?" Lorna said.

Claudia had the grace to look sheepish. "The situations aren't alike."

"No, but there *are* some similarities," Amy pointed out. She blew a strand of hair out of her eyes. "After all, you didn't lay all *your* cards on the table."

"Actually, I did. When John came to plead Philip's case, I told John I wasn't in love with Philip. That I loved someone else." She smiled. "He got the picture."

"You know, Lorna," Amy said. "I think Claudia's got the right idea."

"*You* think I should tell Nick, too?"

"Yes, I do. Don't make a big deal out of it. Bring it up casually. By his reaction, you'll have a pretty good idea of how he feels about you." She grinned. "I'll lay you odds he'll declare himself. Because he's *very* interested in you. That was obvious to anyone with eyes last weekend."

"I don't know. It seems kind of juvenile to tell him, don't you think? Like I'm trying to make him jealous or something."

"That's not juvenile," Claudia said. "Women have been using jealousy in the war between the sexes from the dawn of time. Shoot, it's probably rule number one of 'How To Land Your Man'."

Amy laughed. "Is there such a book?"

Claudia grinned. "If there's not, there should be."

Just then Susan, followed by Stella and Calista,

came bursting into the kitchen. "Mom," Susan shouted, "can we have some ice cream?"

"Please, Mommy, say yes," Calista said.

"*May* we have some ice cream," Amy corrected, "and, yes, you may."

With the children present, the subject of Lorna's love life—or lack of one—was dropped. But Lorna continued to think about what her sister and sister-in-law had advised, and she finally decided maybe they were right. Maybe she *should* tell Nick about Coach. It couldn't do any harm.

And yet the possibility that Nick didn't care and would even urge her to meet Coach scared her. Even so, it was better to know the truth.

Because if Nick *wasn't* going to be a part of her future, she needed to figure out how to survive without him.

Nick was glad Lorna had decided to go to Morgan Creek for the weekend, because it was getting harder and harder to stay away from her. He'd been trying to give her space because he knew she needed to think without any undue influence from him. This decision about Coach was too important. He wanted to be sure when she made it, she'd made it on her own.

But on Monday, he couldn't avoid her company any longer. He'd promised Bryce an expansion plan proposal by the end of the week, and he needed her input. So Monday morning at nine, he walked down to her office.

"Hi, Marilyn."

Lorna's secretary stopped typing and looked at him over the top of her glasses. "Hello, Nick."

"Is she in?" He inclined his head toward Lorna's closed door.

"Yes."

Walking over, he knocked on the door.

"Come in," Lorna called out.

He opened the door. Lorna's welcoming smile didn't falter. A good sign, he thought. "Got a minute?"

"Sure."

He closed the door behind him and took a seat in one of the chairs flanking her desk. She looked exceptionally pretty today, he thought. But then, he wasn't an impartial observer. "How was your trip?"

"Good. It was a relaxing weekend."

"How's Claudia doing?"

"Really well. You'd never know there was ever any question about the baby. She looks wonderful and said she feels wonderful."

"That's good."

She nodded. "But you didn't come to talk about my weekend."

"No, I was hoping you'd be free this afternoon so

we could go over the proposed expansion plan. Cal and I have gone as far as we can, but now I need you to crunch some numbers for me."

She looked at her calendar. "I've got an appointment with that reporter from *Houston Magazine* at one, but I should be free by two-thirty or so."

Nick frowned. "What reporter?"

"Didn't Karen tell you? The magazine wants to do a feature about us for their spring business report issue."

"She may have mentioned it." He grinned. "I probably wasn't paying attention. Okay, two-thirty it is. If you're done sooner, just let me know." He got up. "It may turn into a late night. Is that okay?"

"Sure, no problem."

He was smiling as he walked back to the office. He had a good feeling about tonight.

I'm going to do it, Lorna thought. *Maybe it's not kosher, but I'm going to do it, anyway.*

She waited until they'd finished everything they could possibly do regarding the expansion proposal. Then, as Nick cleared off his desk, she said casually, "You know the guy I write to online? The one who stood me up that day at the Galleria?"

Nick looked up. "Yeah?"

Oh, God. All she had to do was look into his eyes,

and she felt weak in the knees. Good thing she was sitting down. "He wants to meet me again."

"Oh?"

"Yes. He…" She swallowed. "He said he had fallen in love with me."

Nick didn't say anything, just continued to look at her.

If only she knew what he was thinking. "Anyway, I was wondering what you thought about it."

"What *I* thought about it?"

"Yes, you know, a man's opinion. What do you think? Do you think I should go?"

He shrugged. "I can't tell you what to do, Lorna. That has to be your decision. If you want to meet him, then you should go. If not, tell him to take a hike."

Disappointment flooded Lorna. He hadn't even blinked when she'd told him what Coach had said. There could only be one reason for his dispassionate response. He didn't care. It didn't matter in the least to him whether she met Coach or not.

Trying not to let her unhappiness show, she said crisply, "You're right. It *is* my decision."

How stupid you are. You really thought he was going to say he loved you and that he didn't want you to go. Well, he didn't say it because he doesn't *love you. You were a fool to even* think *he might.*

She remembered how once, during an argument,

Keith had told her she didn't turn him on at all, that tall, skinny women weren't sexy.

Even your money wasn't enough to hold him.

Forcing herself to keep her tone light, to not give away how devastated she felt inside, she said, "Well, I've decided. I'm going to meet him." She stood. "In fact, I think I'll write him tonight and tell him so." Then, because she was so hurt, she added, "Who knows? He may turn out to be the man of my dreams."

Nick didn't say anything for a long moment. When he did speak, his voice was expressionless. "I hope your fantasy lover doesn't disappoint you."

Lorna managed to keep from bursting into tears until she reached the parking lot. But then she could no longer hold them inside. She cried her heart out all the way home and she kept crying after crawling into bed.

The tears didn't stop until she finally fell asleep at midnight.

FROM: SweetStuff@jamboree.net
TO: Coach1012@bayoucity.net
SUBJECT: Meeting
Dear Coach,
I've been thinking about what you said all week, and I've finally made up my mind. I'm ready to meet you. When and where?
Love,
Sweet Stuff

FROM: Coach1012@bayoucity.net
TO: SweetStuff@jamboree.net
SUBJECT: Re: Meeting
Dear Sweet Stuff,
I was just thinking about you when your e-mail
came. How about this Saturday? You pick the time
and place. I'm free all day.
Love,
Coach

Lorna wrote back to say she'd meet him at ten
o'clock Saturday morning in front of the Waterwall
by the Williams Tower. This time I'll be wearing
jeans and a red sweater and I'll be carrying another bag of Hathaway cookies.

She waited a few minutes after sending the e-mail
to see if he'd answer. Sure enough, an answer came
through almost immediately.

Sounds good. BTW, I'll have Maggie with me,
he wrote, so you won't be able to miss me.

She stared at the screen. Maybe Nick didn't want
her, but Coach did. And he was a wonderful man.
She'd made the right decision.

So why did she still feel so miserable?

After sending off the e-mail saying he'd bring
Maggie with him on Saturday, Nick knew he had to

get out of the house. If he stayed there, all he'd do was sit and brood. Not a good idea.

He hurriedly dressed in his running clothes, then set out for Memorial Park. It was a good night for running, with temperatures in the low sixties and only forty-percent humidity. Nick loved Houston's weather from October through April. It was only in May, when the temperature and humidity both started to climb, that he started thinking longingly of mountains and cooler climes.

He ran hard and tried not to think at all. For the most part, he was successful, but once he'd finished his workout and was on his way home, his traitorous mind once again turned to Lorna.

He had no idea what Saturday would bring. He wished with all his heart she had told Coach no. Then Nick would have known exactly what to do. As Coach, he would have questioned her, probably come right out and asked her if she was in love with someone else. If she'd given any indication at all that the Nick she knew was more important to her than her online fantasy, Nick would have revealed himself then and there.

But she hadn't.

So where did that leave him?

Lorna wasn't sure she was going to make it through the week without coming unglued. She snapped at Marilyn twice, then had to apologize. She cried when she heard a love song of any kind on the radio. And she told Claudia to mind her own business when Claudia tried to talk to her about what had happened.

"If I hadn't listened to you, maybe things would be all right!" she cried. She knew it was ridiculous to blame Claudia because Nick didn't love her, and she felt bad immediately and told Claudia she was sorry.

"It's okay, Lorna. I know you're upset. I understand."

"How *could* you? You've always known how John felt about you."

"No, I only *hoped* he loved me the way I loved him, but I didn't *know*," Claudia said. "Believe me, I do understand. Any woman who's ever been in love and scared that she's not loved in return understands how you feel."

But Lorna wouldn't be comforted. She was so miserable—more miserable even than when Keith had betrayed her. She was sure no one else had *ever* felt this bad and lived to tell about it.

At least a dozen times throughout the week she thought about writing to Coach and telling him she'd changed her mind. But she didn't. What was the point? Not meeting Coach wasn't going to change anything as far as Nick was concerned. If she'd had any doubts about his motive for not being willing to tell her not to meet Coach, those doubts were dispelled by his behavior since then.

If he'd spent the week avoiding her, she might have still had a smidgen of hope. But he hadn't. He'd been perfectly civil, even friendly, to her every time he'd seen her either in the office wing or on the plant floor. Twice he'd come to her office to ask her a question.

No. Her upcoming meeting with Coach didn't bother Nick at all. There was no hope.

On Saturday morning, Lorna looked out the window to see the sun shining. It was going to be a perfectly gorgeous day—the kind of October day that beckoned to Houstonians to find something to do outdoors.

Lorna almost wished it had rained. Then she'd have a reason to cancel her date with Coach.

Telling herself everything would be fine—she'd made the right decision, now all she had to do was stick with it—she took her coffee into the bathroom and began getting ready.

She knew she might have trouble finding a place to park near the Waterwall, so she arrived early. As feared, she had to drive around the block a couple of times before a place opened up on a side street nearby. She parked, locked the car and waited to cross Post Oak Boulevard. The area was drenched in sunlight. Such a beautiful day, she thought. If only it were Nick she was meeting, everything would be perfect.

Stop it. Stop wishing for the moon.

Once she'd crossed the busy thoroughfare, she stood for a moment looking up. The Tower always fascinated her. Built in 1983, it was first called the Transco Tower, but the name had been changed a few years back when the Williams family purchased the building. It was the tallest building outside of a major metropolitan area and one of the city's best known and most impressive landmarks.

The Waterwall stood behind it and had been a magnet for visitors ever since it had been built. Children especially adored coming to see it. They'd stand on the steps and let the fine mist cool them on hot summer days.

Lorna sighed and slowly walked toward the steps herself. There were several adults and a couple of children there. She looked at the lone man and knew immediately he wasn't Coach because he stood with his arm around a pretty dark-haired woman whose head rested on his shoulder as they gazed at the water cascading down the wall.

Walking up to the third step, Lorna paused and turned to face the street so she could see anyone approaching. Glancing at her watch, she saw it was only eight minutes to ten. She might have a while to wait. She took a deep breath to calm herself.

This upcoming meeting was so different from the first one at the Galleria. Then she'd been excited and anxious to meet Coach. She'd been filled with anticipation and hope.

Today she was filled with despair.

And no matter how many times she told herself she was doing the right thing, it didn't *feel* like the right thing. The truth was, she no longer had any desire to move forward into a different kind of relationship with Coach. It didn't matter if he was the most handsome, wonderful man on earth. He no longer held romantic appeal.

Nick was the only man who interested her.

The only man she wanted.

Now fighting tears, she knew she'd made a terrible mistake. She had to get out of here.

Almost stumbling in her haste to get down the steps and away before Coach arrived, she almost ran headlong into a man who was approaching from the street.

"Oh, I'm sorry—" she began, then looked up.

Lorna had never believed a heart could actually stop, but in that moment, hers did. For standing before her, looking impossibly handsome, stood Nick.

"Where are you going?" he said.

For a moment, no words would come. "Wh-what are *you* doing here?"

His dark gaze bore into hers. "Answer my question first."

Deciding to abandon the safety of the guardrail

around her heart, Lorna leaped. "I don't belong here. I realized I don't want to meet him."

"Why not?" Nick asked softly. His eyes still pinned hers.

"Because he's not the man I want."

"Am I the man you want?"

"Yes."

And then, in a moment Lorna knew she would remember until the day she took her last breath, she belatedly spied the dog that sat quietly next to Nick. A beautiful chocolate Lab who looked at her just as intently as its owner. Lorna's gaze flew to Nick's.

He smiled. Then, still holding her gaze, he said, "Maggie, meet Sweet Stuff, the woman I love."

"Oh," Lorna said. She was utterly incapable of saying anything else. Her mind whirled crazily. Yet one fact emerged clearly. Nick was Coach!

A moment later, she was in his arms.

"Don't cry," he whispered, kissing her wet eyes. "Don't cry."

"I can't help it. I'm so happy."

When his mouth settled against hers, heat exploded inside her, and she felt she might burst with happiness. She didn't care that they were standing in the middle of a public area and that there were people all around watching them. All she cared about was that she was with Nick, that he loved her and that he was showing the world how he felt.

The kiss lasted a long time. When he finally raised his head, he said, "Let's get out of here." His voice was husky.

She nodded.

Maggie barked.

Nick laughed. "Maggie's ready to go, too. Where's your car?"

"Over there." Lorna pointed to the side street.

"That's where I parked, too."

Arms around each other, they walked to Lorna's truck. Once there, Nick waited until she was inside and ready to go. "Follow me to my house?" he said.

She could see in his eyes that when they got there, they were going to make love.

The realization gave her a hollow feeling, and her heart skittered. What if she disappointed him? He'd had a lot of experience, and she'd had so little.

But she pushed her doubts away and took her second huge leap of the day. "I'd follow you anywhere," she said.

Chapter Thirteen

Lorna had forgotten how wonderful it was to touch and be touched. To connect, in this most intimate way, with someone you loved. To feel both tenderness and passion, love and desire. This was better than any dream she'd ever had, any fantasy. This was the best life had to offer. This was what life was all about.

Nick was a wonderful lover—thoughtful and generous. Lying in his big bed striped by the sunlight that peeked through the slatted blinds, Lorna gave herself up to the intense sweetness and wonder that filled her. She reveled in the awakening of her senses, trembled as he feathered kisses everywhere. He began at her earlobe, moved slowly down to her neck and across her breasts, then glided down to her belly, all the while stroking her and whispering to her and telling her how beautiful she was.

She shivered under his touch, moaned softly as he explored all her secret places.

When he finally raised his head to capture her mouth with his, she could taste herself on him, and the desire that had been building suddenly exploded.

"Now," she said, digging her nails into his back.

When he entered her, plunging deep, she cried out.

"I'm not hurting you, am I?" he gasped.

"No, no." She wrapped her legs around him and urged him even deeper. She wanted all of him. She wanted everything. She wanted to stay this way forever.

Together they found their unique rhythm and, moving as one, began the ascent toward that yearned-for pinnacle. Their need for each other grew as they climbed higher and higher. Finally they were there, at the top. Lorna felt as if her body were falling apart as wave after wave of intense pleasure shuddered through her. Moments later, Nick cried out with his own release, and as she held him tight, she closed her eyes and thanked God for answering her prayers.

When their hearts calmed and their bodies cooled, Nick gathered her to him spoon fashion. "I love you," he murmured. One hand lazily cupped her breast. The other stroked her hip.

Lorna sighed deeply. "I love you, too," she murmured back. She could have stayed here, in his bed, forever. Maybe she would.

From somewhere outside, she could hear the faint sounds of children at play. She closed her eyes.

For a while, they dozed.

When they awoke, they slowly began to make love again. This time, Lorna explored Nick's body, giving it the minute and careful attention he'd given her earlier. She found she was just as aroused by watching him and touching him and hearing his moans as she had been when he'd been the aggressor.

And when he gasped, saying he couldn't wait another minute, she climbed on top and lowered herself onto him. She watched as he tried to hold off and couldn't. To know she had the power to give him so much pleasure only intensified her own.

Later, they played the game all lovers play.

"When did you first realize you loved me?" she said, running her fingers through his curly chest hair.

He chuckled. "When I saw you in Memorial Park, all sweaty and smelly, and still wanted to kiss you."

Lorna pinched him.

"Ow!"

"That's what you get for calling me all sweaty and smelly."

"The truth hurts sometimes."

"No, seriously…when *did* you?"

His voice softened. "I think I knew, on some level, the day I saw you at the Galleria and couldn't leave you there waiting for Coach, who would never come." He rolled over on his side and kissed the tip of her nose. "What about you? When did you stop hating me?"

"I never hated you," she said softly.

"You sure didn't love me."

"No, not at first."

"So when *did* you know?"

"I think I knew the day you brought me flowers and soup." She snuggled closer to him.

"So after that you were playing hard to get?" he teased.

They continued their lighthearted banter, which turned into tickling, which turned into a pillow fight, which turned into Nick chasing Lorna through the house.

Afterward, laughing so hard she was almost crying, Lorna confessed her behavior was very uncharacteristic. "You're bringing out the bad girl in me."

"Lucky me," Nick said, backing her up to a wall and kissing her. "I hope you stay bad forever." He kissed her again.

Which led to more lovemaking.

"My family is going to be shocked when they see you walk in the door," Nick said.

"Nick! You mean you didn't call your mother and tell her I was coming?" It was Sunday. Lorna had spent the night at Nick's and now they were at her house while she got ready to meet his family.

"Nope." He grinned. "I wanted to surprise them."

Lorna couldn't believe it. "But won't she be *furious* with you?" She thought about how her own mother wanted plenty of warning when guests were on the way so that everything could be perfect when they arrived.

"Nah. My mother's cool that way. 'The more the merrier' has always been her motto."

"Do I look all right?" She had agonized over what to wear, finally settling on dressy black pants and a pale blue sweater set. She so wanted them to like her. What if they *didn't* like her? "Maybe I should wear a dress."

Now Nick laughed. "Lorna, you look beautiful. Quit worrying. They're going to love you." He slipped his arms around her waist and nibbled on her ear. "*I* love you," he whispered, one hand moving down to caress her bottom.

"Stop that," she said with a breathy chuckle.

"Why?" he whispered, his hand becoming bolder.

"Because we'll be late if we keep this up." But she was smiling, thinking of yesterday and how they'd made love four times, the last time in the shower, which was every bit as wonderful and decadent and unbelievably sexy as Lorna had ever fantasized it would be.

"You're no fun."

She grinned. "Later, okay?"

"I'm going to hold you to that."

"I hope so."

Nick's parents still lived in the same northwest neighborhood where he had grown up, he told Lorna once they were on their way. "It's not a fancy house," he warned.

"What makes you think I care about fancy?"

He glanced over at her and smiled. "Sorry. I know you don't."

It took her a while to reply. When she did her voice was thoughtful. "Does the fact that I have money bother you, Nick?"

His first instinct was to say no. But if he wanted her to be honest with him in all things, he had to be honest with her. "Yeah, it does." He smiled ruefully. "It almost kept me from pursuing a relationship with you."

"But why? What difference does it make that I have money? You're a successful man with a responsible job that I had nothing to do with and you have a beautiful home."

"I know, but… Oh, hell, Lorna, we're not exactly on the same social level, and whatever success I've achieved is nothing compared to your family's accomplishments."

"Social level," she scoffed. "What does *that* mean, for heaven's sake? Believe me, Nick, I don't come from an aristocratic family, no matter *what* my grandmother and mother would have you believe. My ancestors were pioneers who worked the land for a living. And my great-great grandfather, the one who founded Hathaway Baking, was just a simple baker who started with one small place and got lucky."

"That kind of success takes more than luck."

"Well, yes, he *worked* hard, and so did the Hathaways who came after him, but my point is, we're not special people. We're *fortunate* people, but we're no better than anyone else. We're certainly not better than your family."

Nick knew what she was saying made sense, but there was still a part of him that would never feel comfortable with her level of wealth.

"Look, Nick," she went on, "I know you don't want me for my money, and that means the world to me. Honestly, if I thought my money would drive a wedge between us, I'd give it all away."

He smiled at that. He had a feeling she meant it. Reaching over, he laid his hand on her thigh and gently squeezed. "Knowing that means the world to *me*," he said softly. Then he laughed. "But you don't have to give away your money. I can live with having a wealthy wife."

"Wife?"

Nick could have kicked himself. He'd meant to propose after he'd had a chance to buy her a ring. And here they were, in the car, of all places. "Um, that was a slip of the tongue. I don't guess you could forget what I said until I can do this properly?"

She laughed. "Not on your life."

"Okay, okay." Coming to a side street, he turned onto it, then pulled over to the curb and cut the ignition. Turning to face her, he reached for her hand. "Lorna, I love you, and I want to spend the rest of my life with you. Will you do me the honor of becoming Mrs. DeSanto?"

Her eyes filled with tears. "Oh, Nick, I want that more than anything. But—"

"But what?" Suddenly he was scared. "But what?" he said more firmly.

She bit her lip. "But what if I can't give you children? I mean, I didn't get pregnant when I was married to Keith, no matter how hard I tried or how much I wanted to. What if the same thing happens with us?" Her eyes were tormented as they met his.

"It doesn't matter. We'll adopt."

"Oh, Nick."

"Look, Lorna, I love you. Yes, I'd like for us to have kids, but if it doesn't happen, it doesn't. I still want to marry you. Now what do you say?"

Now she was really crying. "I say yes!"

It wasn't easy to kiss with the gearshift between them, but they did a pretty good job of it. When they broke apart, he said, "Can we tell my family today or do you want to tell yours first?"

"Let's tell them today."

"Damn, I wish I had a ring for you."

"I don't need a ring."

"I'm going to buy you one, Lorna. I was going to go pick one out tomorrow night."

Her eyes were still watery, but shining with happiness. "Now we can do it together."

By the time they reached his parents' house, Nick knew even if they *weren't* planning to tell his family their news, one look at his and Lorna's faces, and they'd have guessed it, anyway.

Lorna immediately loved Nick's parents. Carmela was everything she'd imagined his mother to be: warm, pretty, smart and funny. And Mike, Nick's dad, was just an older version of Nick: same dark eyes, same dark hair (what was left of it), same good looks and the same confidence that just seemed a natural part of him. He also had a great sense of humor and loved to tease.

His brothers, too, were exactly what she'd have pictured. And, of course, she'd met Marie.

She could tell they were all shocked to see her

walk in with Nick, but they recovered quickly, saying how nice it was to meet her, and how glad they were that Nicky had brought her to dinner.

Carmela hurriedly set another plate at the large dining room table, and Nick's father brought her a glass of wine and asked her how she liked living in Houston. When Nick came and sat next to her on the sofa in the family room, he reached for her hand, and she gratefully clasped it.

Would he tell them now? she wondered. She could see that they'd noticed he was holding her hand, even though they were trying to act as if this was the most normal occurrence in the world. Lorna knew it wasn't. In fact, Nick had told her he hadn't brought a girl home to meet his parents since he was in high school.

He waited until they were all seated at the table and his father had finished saying grace. Then Nick stood. "Before we begin eating, I have something to tell you. *We* have something to tell you." Reaching for Lorna's hand, he drew her up alongside him. "Today Lorna has made me a happy man." He turned to smile down into her eyes. "She's consented to become my wife."

His mother gasped, and Marie's eyes went wide.

"Oh, Nicky!" his mother said. "Oh, I'm so *happy* for you!"

Lorna hadn't realized she'd been holding her

breath until she expelled it. Smiles and good wishes rained down upon them, and once again, she felt herself close to tears. To think she would soon belong to this loving family. She was so lucky. So very lucky.

When everyone had settled down, the questions began.

"I thought you said you two weren't even dating," Marie said. "Not that I believed you for a minute."

Nick laughed. "We *weren't* dating." He looked at Lorna. "Were we?"

"Not exactly."

"You're talking in riddles," Nick's mother said. "If you weren't dating, then how…?" Her voice trailed off.

So Nick told them how he and Lorna had met online. He didn't tell them everything, for which Lorna was grateful, but he told them enough so that they got the picture.

"Oh, that's *so* romantic," Jay's wife Kathy said. At least Lorna thought she was Jay's wife and not Mike Jr.'s. Must be. She looked younger than Candy.

"And you didn't know this guy you were involved with online was actually Nick?" Marie said.

Lorna shook her head.

"But *you* found out a while ago," Marie said to Nick.

He smiled. "Yes."

By now they'd begun to pass the lasagne and salad and other side dishes.

"Did you know that night I saw you at Chuck's?"

"Yes."

"Why, you stinker," Marie said. "And you were so adamant that the two of you weren't dating. I *knew* you weren't telling the truth."

Lorna wanted to say that they'd never really dated, but she decided it didn't matter what his family thought. All that mattered was that they had found each other. That they loved each other and were going to be married.

Nothing else was important.

Telling Lorna's family was even easier. Bryce already liked and respected Nick, and Amy had fallen prey to his charms the first time she met him. So they were both tickled. Claudia and John liked him, too, so they were pleased and happy for Lorna.

Her mother, who might have given Lorna some grief last year, was now in no position to object to Lorna's choice. But Lorna didn't think she would have, anyway. As she'd told Nick, he was a successful man in his own right. He didn't need to take a back seat to anyone.

The only time Lorna was nervous was when they told her grandmother Stella. She knew how imperious the older woman could be. As Lorna made the introductions, her grandmother looked Nick up and down, then she questioned him thoroughly. Through it all, Nick was charming and courteous, but he didn't grovel.

"Young man," Lorna's grandmother finally said, "I think you'll do."

Nick smiled. "Thank you, Mrs. Hathaway."

"The truth is, you remind me of my husband when he was young."

Lorna bit back a smile. This was the ultimate compliment.

"Just make sure you're good to my granddaughter."

Nick looked at Lorna. "That won't be hard. She's pretty special."

"Yes, she is, and don't you forget it."

When they left, Nick was laughing. "She's one of a kind, isn't she?"

"You could say that."

"I'm glad she approved of me."

"Me, too."

"Would you still marry me even if she didn't approve?"

"What do *you* think?"

"I think you'd better say yes."

"Or?" Lorna said, laughing.

"Or…you'll be sorry."

Now Lorna was really laughing. "Is that the best you can do? I thought maybe you'd threaten to throw me over your shoulder and carry me off like some Neanderthal."

"That *does* sound like fun," Nick said.

By now they'd reached Bryce's house, where they were going to have dinner. Nick pulled Lorna behind one of the big oleander bushes that grew on one side of the house and once they were hidden from view, he kissed her hungrily. "I'm glad we're staying at a hotel tonight," he said when they came up for air. "Because I can't get enough of you."

Lorna decided if she died then and there, she'd die a happy woman.

Both Lorna and Nick wanted a small wedding, but they knew it was a futile wish. Unless they wanted to elope the way Claudia and John had, they were going to have to bite the bullet and let their families have their way.

Lorna might have opted for an elopement, but she didn't want to disappoint her grandmother again. Grandmother Stella was still hurt over Claudia's and Lorna's leaving Morgan Creek. Then Claudia's elopement had added another blow. If Lorna refused a "real" wedding—as her grandmother persisted in calling it—she would hurt her needlessly.

So she and Nick would be married at the First Methodist Church in Morgan Creek where her grandmother had been a member her entire life.

Amy was going to be Lorna's matron of honor and Claudia and Chloe would be bridesmaids. Chloe's daughter Cameron would be a junior bridesmaid, and Stella, Susan and Calista would be flower girls.

Nick's brother Mike would be his best man. Jay and Bryce and his brother-in-law Rich and Claudia's husband John would serve as groomsmen.

The reception would be held at the Morgan Creek Country Club and more than three hundred invitations had been sent. The wedding ceremony would take place at five o'clock in the evening the second Saturday of December. The only real ruckus had been over the date. Lorna's grandmother wanted them to wait until spring, saying, "It's unseemly to get married so quickly. People will think you're pregnant or something."

But Nick and Lorna had been insistent on that point. Neither wanted to wait. When Lorna said, only half teasing, that maybe they should elope, her grandmother had given in, but she'd pouted for days. She didn't like not getting her own way.

After the ceremony, there would be an hour of cocktails at the club while the photographer took pictures of the wedding party and family, then the doors to the dining room would open, and there would be a sit-down dinner for all the guests. After dinner, an orchestra would play for dancing until the wee hours of the morning.

Lorna and Nick planned to leave the reception no later than midnight, because the next day they were flying to Rome for a three-week honeymoon in Italy. Nick planned to take Lorna to the little town near Naples where his DeSanto ancestors had come from.

Lorna's grandmother had had Bryce's secretary reserve all the rooms that were available at the local hotel from the Thursday before the wedding through the Monday afterward so that any out of town guests that couldn't be accommodated in the Hathaway mansion would have a comfortable place to stay.

Claudia helped Lorna shop for a suitable gown. Claudia thought Lorna should wear white, or at least off-white. But Lorna was firm. "I've been married before," she said. "White is not appropriate."

"Oh, who follows those silly rules, anyway," Claudia grumbled.

"Gran does. So as long as I'm doing this big wedding to please her and Nick's family, I might as well go all the way."

"So what color were you thinking of?"

"A very pale pink."

Claudia grinned. "That's pretty close to white, you know."

Lorna had a definite idea of the kind of dress she wanted. And they found the perfect gown at one of the exclusive shops in Houston. A Vera Wang design, it was made of heavy satin with a narrow waist and gently flowing skirt. The deep V neckline and scalloped hemline were both trimmed with tiny rosettes studded with brilliants. Lorna fell in love with the dress at first sight and realized how lucky she was to be able to afford it.

For the female attendants, Lorna chose long dresses made from a dusty rose velvet. The little girls were wearing white taffeta with a rose satin sash.

At first Amy was disappointed when she heard the color scheme. "Since it'll be so close to Christmas, I thought you'd choose Christmas colors."

Lorna shook her head. "I'm going to carry pink roses, so red and green wouldn't have worked."

Lorna left Houston for Morgan Creek a week before the wedding. Nick would follow after his bachelor party, which was going to take place Wednesday night.

The day of the wedding dawned clear, bright and cold. A perfect day, Lorna thought, looking out the window toward Bryce's house. She would not see Nick today. They were keeping to the tradition of not seeing each other until they arrived at the church. Lorna raised her left hand, holding it in the shaft of sunlight that streamed into the window. The large marquise-cut diamond that Nick had given her sparkled with a fiery brilliance that almost hurt her eyes.

Oh, she was so happy! she thought. Nothing could take away from that happiness. Not the tense looks she'd noticed between Chloe and her husband last night at the party her mother had hosted for the two families. Not the little drama that had played out between her mother and her grandmother over who would be the last one seated before the bridal procession began. Her grandmother had won that one, of course. It hadn't even been a contest.

No, nothing other than Nick and the fact she would, in less than eight hours, be Mrs. Nick De Santo was important today. Lorna was still standing at the window daydreaming when there was a knock at her bedroom door.

Grabbing her robe, she put it on, then walked over and opened the door. Her grandmother, fully dressed and sitting in her wheelchair, smiled up at her.

"Good morning, Lorna," she said. "Did I wake you?" Without waiting to be invited, she wheeled herself in.

"Good morning, Grandmother. No, you didn't wake me. I was up."

"Please close the door, Lorna. I have something to tell you and something to give you, and I would like for us to have privacy."

Lorna felt a tiny flutter of alarm. Her grandmother sounded so serious.

"First of all, I wanted to tell you that I am very proud of you, my dear. You are a wonderful young woman, and I love you very much."

"Oh, Gran, I love you, too. And thank you for saying you're proud of me. That means a lot to me." Lorna bent down and kissed her grandmother's soft, crepey cheek. As always, her grandmother smelled of the Joy she had used for as long as Lorna could remember.

"Sit down, my dear, would you? I have a confession to make, and I'll be more comfortable looking you in the eye rather than having you tower over me."

"I'm sorry, Gran." Lorna sat on the edge of the bed. A confession? What could her grandmother possibly have to confess that would cause her discomfort, for now that Lorna looked closer, she could see that her grandmother was agitated. "What is it, Gran?"

"You know I never liked Keith."

Lorna blinked. "Yes. You told me that when I told you I was filing for divorce."

"Well, after you divorced him, I hired a private investigator to do some checking on him."

"Checking?"

"Yes. Specifically, I asked the investigator to delve into Keith's medical history."

Now Lorna was thoroughly confused. "His medical history?" she repeated. "What for?"

"Because I wanted to know if he was sterile. I suspected he might have lied to you because he didn't want you to know *he* was the one at fault when it came to your not being able to conceive. After all, we knew it wasn't *your* fault. Your gynecologist confirmed that."

Lorna nodded. That's what she'd been told, but the

fact was, she hadn't been able to get pregnant, and Keith had assured her—many times—that his doctor had said his sperm count was high. She still remembered how he'd looked at her when he'd told her, as if he'd always known she was inadequate.

"Anyway," her grandmother continued, "Mr. Cooke—that's the investigator's name—found out something extremely interesting." She paused for a moment. Her blue eyes, still bright, still shrewd, met Lorna's squarely. "Keith had a vasectomy the week after you returned from your honeymoon."

If her grandmother had dropped a bomb in the room, it couldn't have shaken Lorna more. A vasectomy! Keith had had a vasectomy. The words pummeled Lorna. "You mean," she said slowly, "all those years when I was agonizing and thinking there had to be something wrong with me because I couldn't get pregnant, he was…he'd had…a vasectomy? H-how long have you known this?"

"For a while now."

"But why didn't you *tell* me?"

"I wanted to wait for the right time."

Lorna would never understand her grandmother, and yet, did it matter that she hadn't told her until now? Wasn't the important thing that she'd found out something Lorna might never have known otherwise? "Oh, Gran, this is the best gift anyone could ever have given me today." She bent over and kissed her grandmother again. "Thank you. Thank you from the bottom of my heart."

Lorna was shocked to see a tear roll down her grandmother's cheek. Her grandmother never cried. Never. This touched Lorna more than anything could have.

"I have something else for you," her grandmother said, wiping the tear away. She looked almost embarrassed.

It was only then Lorna noticed the flat gray velvet box in her grandmother's lap. Her grandmother picked it up and handed it to Lorna. "They were my mother's and now I want you to have them."

Lorna snapped open the lid and sucked in her breath. Inside lay her great-grandmother Eleanor's diamond choker and matching earrings. "Oh, they're so beautiful," she said. "But shouldn't they go to Chloe?"

"I don't like Greg, either."

Lorna couldn't help it. She started to laugh. Her grandmother was definitely one of a kind. "I take it that means you like Nick."

"I told you. He reminds me of your grandfather. Now, promise me you'll wear the diamonds today. They can be your something old."

"I will wear them today and treasure them always," Lorna said. But the other gift, the knowledge that it had never been her fault she couldn't get pregnant, that was the most precious gift her grandmother had given her today. Aside from Nick, it was the most precious gift she'd ever been given.

So at five o'clock that afternoon, amid hundreds of flickering candles and the fragrance of dozens and dozens of roses, Lorna slowly walked down the aisle of the First Methodist Church toward the man she would promise to love and cherish for the rest of her life. She was wearing the beautiful diamonds that had belonged to her great-grandmother and hugging the knowledge close to her heart that, if they were lucky, she might already be carrying the fruit of their love.

Her eyes met Nick's as she reached the altar. He smiled, and she smiled back. Then she placed her hand in his, and together they faced the minister, and the wedding ceremony began.

Epilogue

Fourteen months later...

"Oh, Lorna, he's such a beautiful baby!" Amy exclaimed.

Lorna beamed with pride as she studied her six-month-old son. Nicholas Hathaway DeSanto. He *was* a beautiful baby. Strong and lusty, he had made his presence known from the instant he'd been delivered from the warmth of her womb to the outside world. He had his father's dark hair and her blue eyes and her Grandmother Stella's stubborn belief that anything she wanted she would get if she only made enough noise.

"Just think, you've produced the first boy in to the Hathaway family since your father was born."

Lorna smiled. This was true. Claudia had given birth to a little girl they had named Camille. Claudia was pregnant again, but she told Lorna she just had a feeling she was going to have another girl.

"Oh, Nicky," Lorna said, nuzzling her son's fat neck and breathing in the wonderful baby smell, "you're going to be *so* spoiled."

"Who's going to be so spoiled?"

Lorna turned at the sound of her husband's voice. "You know who. Your pride and joy here."

"He's already spoiled," Nick pointed out.

Amy laughed.

As her husband took the baby from her arms and did a bit of nuzzling of his own, causing little Nick to gurgle with laughter, Lorna felt such a rush of happiness she was afraid she would burst.

She almost wished Amy wasn't in the room, even though she loved when Bryce and Amy came to visit. *It's okay, though. I can wait,* she thought. *I can wait and tell him tonight, after everyone else is in bed and we're alone in our room.*

She smiled to herself. Until then, she would hug her precious secret close, and enjoy it as her own for just a little longer. But tomorrow, after she'd told Nick and they'd had their own private celebration, they could tell the world that in just seven months, their family was going to once more expand, and little Nick would have a brother or a sister.

Just then, Nick's eyes met hers over the head of their son. In them she saw a love that she knew would endure, no matter what the future held.

She was the luckiest woman in the world.

* * * * *

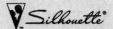

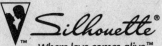

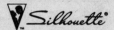

SPECIAL EDITION™

presents the first book in a compelling new miniseries by reader favorite

Christine Flynn

This quiet Vermont town inspires old lovers to reunite—and new loves to blossom!

TRADING SECRETS
SE #1678, available April 2005

Free-spirited, ambitious Jenny Baker thought she'd left Maple Mountain behind forever. But her city life didn't go quite as well as she'd planned, and now Jenny is back home, trying to put her life back together—and trying to keep the truth about her return under wraps. Until she's hired by handsome local doctor Greg Reid, who ignites feelings she'd thought she'd put to rest long ago. And when Greg uncovers Jenny's deepest secret, he makes her an offer she can't refuse....

Where love comes alive™

SSETS

If you enjoyed what you just read,
then we've got an offer you can't resist!

Take 2 bestselling
love stories FREE!
Plus get a FREE surprise gift!

Clip this page and mail it to Silhouette Reader Service™

IN U.S.A.	IN CANADA
3010 Walden Ave.	P.O. Box 609
P.O. Box 1867	Fort Erie, Ontario
Buffalo, N.Y. 14240-1867	L2A 5X3

YES! Please send me 2 free Silhouette Special Edition® novels and my free
surprise gift. After receiving them, if I don't wish to receive anymore, I can return the
shipping statement marked cancel. If I don't cancel, I will receive 6 brand-new novels
every month, before they're available in stores! In the U.S.A., bill me at the bargain
price of $4.24 plus 25¢ shipping and handling per book and applicable sales tax, if
any*. In Canada, bill me at the bargain price of $4.99 plus 25¢ shipping and handling
per book and applicable taxes**. That's the complete price and a savings of at least
10% off the cover prices—what a great deal! I understand that accepting the 2 free
books and gift places me under no obligation ever to buy any books. I can always
return a shipment and cancel at any time. Even if I never buy another book from
Silhouette, the 2 free books and gift are mine to keep forever.

235 SDN DZ9D
335 SDN DZ9E

Name _____ (PLEASE PRINT) _____

Address _____ Apt.# _____

City _____ State/Prov. _____ Zip/Postal Code _____

Not valid to current Silhouette Special Edition® subscribers.

Want to try two free books from another series?
Call 1-800-873-8635 or visit www.morefreebooks.com.

* Terms and prices subject to change without notice. Sales tax applicable in N.Y.
** Canadian residents will be charged applicable provincial taxes and GST.
  All orders subject to approval. Offer limited to one per household.
® are registered trademarks owned and used by the trademark owner and or its licensee.

SPED04R   ©2004 Harlequin Enterprises Limited

SILHOUETTE *Romance*®

*presents a **sassy** new romance*
by Angie Ray

THE MILLIONAIRE'S REWARD

(Silhouette Romance #1764)

Wealthy tycoon Garek Wisnewski is used to
getting what he wants…and he wants new
employee Ellie Hernandez. Garek knows that
the spirited beauty is against mixing business
with pleasure, but this corporate bad boy has a
romantic merger planned, and he won't
let anything—even Ellie's halfhearted
objections—stand in his way.

*Available April 2005
at your favorite retail outlet.*